THE DAY BEFORE TODAY

Lockdown Stories

Gayatri Gill

Illustrations by Niyati Singh

SPEAKING
TIGER

SPEAKING TIGER BOOKS LLP
4381/4, Ansari Road, Daryaganj
New Delhi 110002, India

First published by Speaking Tiger Books 2020

ISBN: 978-93-89958-65-2
eISBN: 978-93-89958-55-3

10 9 8 7 6 5 4 3 2 1

Typeset in Adobe Garamond Pro by Jojy Philip, New Delhi
Printed at Chaman Enterprises, New Delhi

Gayatri Gill is a producer, scriptwriter, story editor and co-founder at Swastik Productions, Mumbai, with over fifteen years of writing and production experience across television, digital, animation and documentary formats. *The Day Before Today* is her debut collection of short fiction.

Mother to two children, two dogs and the occasional reptilian visitor, Gayatri enjoys her morning tea brewed with tales of the dark kind.

Niyati Singh is lead researcher of the India Justice Report at the Tata Trusts. She has an MSc in Refugee and Forced Migration Studies from the University of Oxford. In her spare time, she tries to be artistic, and talk to stray dogs—though never simultaneously.

Praise for THE DAY BEFORE TODAY: LOCKDOWN STORIES

'Edgy, fast-paced and raw, these short stories will chase your Corona lethargy away and make you think. Perfect reading to match your mood during these disturbing yet strangely introspective times.' —Bulbul Sharma, writer and painter.

'Hilariously cynical and twisted. A must-read!'—Vish Dhamija, bestselling author of crime fiction.

'Shards of stories, as brittle as life itself that leave you gasping. Yet wishing for more.'—Paro Anand, award-winning author of children's and YA fiction.

'An electric new voice.'—Shinie Antony, writer and director, Bangalore Literature Festival.

'This is where Handmaiden's Tale meets Woody Allen meets shades of Hitchcock noir! Thematically apposite, razor-sharp prose. A natural, this literary debutante!'—Sunil Mehra, journalist, actor and Dastgangoi artiste.

'With energy, precision, frustration, contained fury and delight, Gayatri Gill zooms through a welter of lives upended by the pandemic with the speed of light and the eye of a practised storyteller, timing her chilling endings (and beginnings) perfectly with tales of love and betrayal, toilets and wailing children but also of a joyful family flying in its kitchen in the dead of night, celebrating togetherness.' —Sanjoy Hazarika, writer and International Director, Commonwealth Human Rights Initative (CHRI).

'Gayatri Gill uses very tiny canvases to etch stories that have a wicked sting in their tales. An entertaining and uncomfortable read.'—Venita Coelho, writer, film director and artist.

'A modern allegorical chronicle of AC times, a time that is going to stay with us, a time that has redefined and underlined a new way of living. A heralder of new age writing, pithy, dark, sour, insightful, intuitive and funnily sweet.'—Pratyaksha, writer and artist.

'Short, sharp tales of how people come to terms with life during lockdown—from cooking to murder—and how prejudice, and hope, refuse to go away.'—Ankush Saikia, writer.

For my grandparents, with love.

CONTENTS

DAY ONE

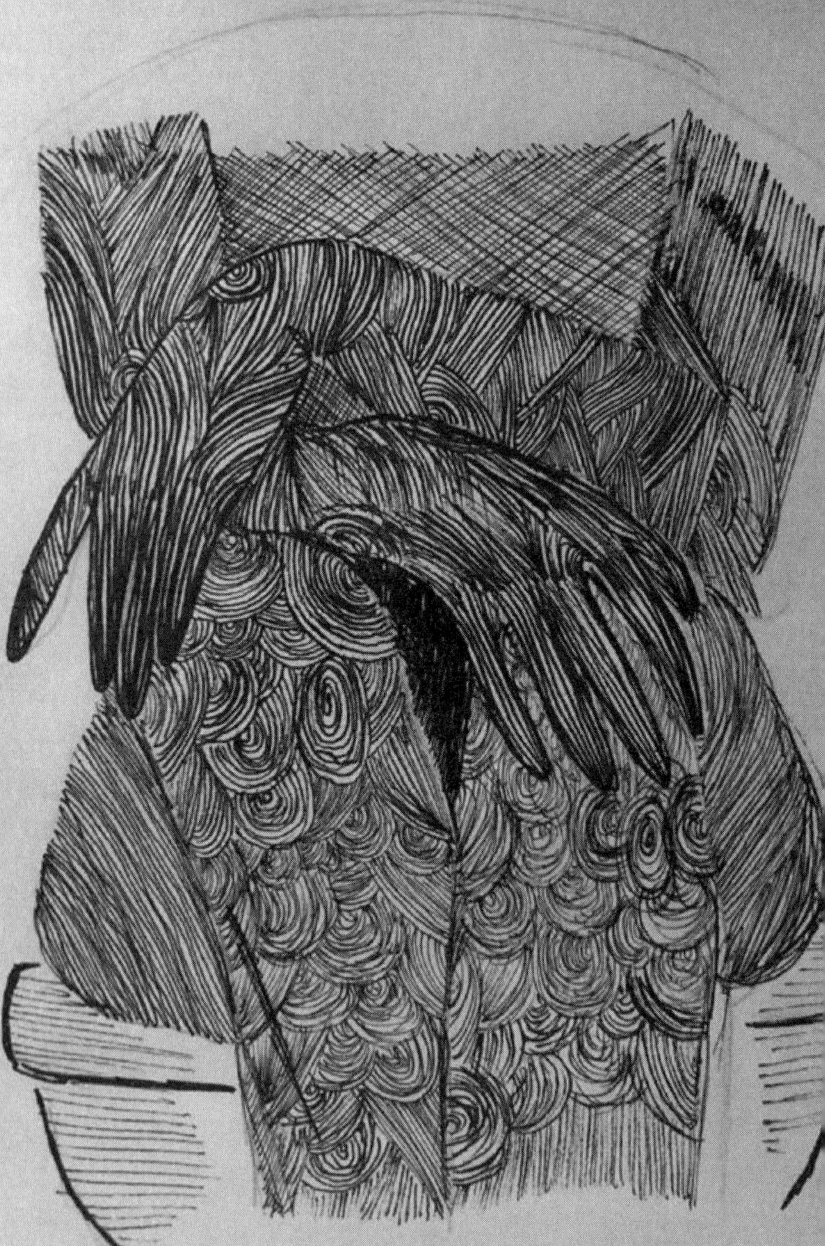

IT WAS A CRAP DAY FROM THE MOMENT IT BEGAN. The morning ablutions weren't satisfactory and that's always a sign of the hours to come. I sat on the pot wishing the screaming toddler at the bathroom door would stop whining and my mother-in-law in the kitchen would stop ranting and the brother-in-law would shut off the damn TV and the dog would stop barking and the neighbours would stop drilling and the cars would stop honking and I could just for the mother of god crap peacefully.

Life hadn't begun this way. It never really does, does it? I was young too once, not the weather-beaten woman with the million squiggly wrinkles round my eyes I see in the mirror today. I had a life, a world and even a love. Several, actually, but the one I chose was clearly not the one for life. He died on me a few years back. That may sound insensitive but fuck you. You're reading my story and since I'm the one writing it, you better hear it my way.

So, let me tell you a thing or two about death. It all starts very easy with the grief and the pain and the endless loss but then it reaches deep into your soul and pulls out your innards. People move on, you know, cupboards get cleaned out, shoes get given away... hell, even his place at the dining table has been taken by the brother-in-law now. They mention him every once in a while, in passing—a fading memory much like the *alu bhaja* your *dadi* used to make. But she's dead now and so you remember the *alu bhaja* as being the greatest delicacy ever made but the truth is that the *alu bhaja* was always just *alu bhaja*—was then and is now. It wasn't the greatest delicacy ever made. That's just your mind playing tricks on you—memory and reflection have a way of reshaping themselves with every repetition. And stories about dead people tend to exaggerate them into sainthood. Beings who must never have walked the earth.

Certainly not walked the dirty garbage-infested bylanes of the colony where our home is. Our home? Correction, his house, which I was married into and am now stuck in because he left. And now I need to spend the rest of my life in memory of a saint who doesn't even sound like my fucking husband. And I can never say that because you don't talk ill of the dead. Not even if it is the truth. And so, you continue to live with the dead. Hoping against hope, wishing with all your bloody might that somehow, somewhere there lies a cure for all your troubles.

The cries of the toddler get more frenzied, the mother-in-law yells for me even louder, the brother-in-law continues watching the telly. FUCK MY LIFE. A feeling of utter helplessness much like I feel every single day because there is no way out. I'M STUCK IN HERE FOREVER AND I WISH AND PRAY that someone somewhere listens to me today and just changes EVERYTHING.

I pull the flush and make for the bathroom door. It's just another day starring me—in my life. And everything stays the same. Always. Until.

Someone somewhere, right at this very moment, is doing something that will get you out of this mess. Something that will change everything. That will destroy the mundanity of everything. Something that will shake everyone up and make them breathe your reality. Something that will trap them and not allow them to get out. Just like you're trapped.

Somewhere far away a bat in a cage stirs in his sleep. He will die tomorrow.

A family a few kilometres away decides to have bat soup for lunch.

POSITIVE

A BRIGHT SUNNY DAY, HOLDING PROMISE OF A HOT approaching summer. The birds chirrup in the distance and social media tells me the pollution levels the world over have halved. Why, there are dolphins swimming in the canals of Venice. Who would've thought! And so today I've decided to be positive. From now onwards I will see only the happiness in it all. Every dark cloud has a silver lining and these apocalyptic times have made everyone so dark and cynical—the news reports, the dying people, the 'I am Legend' movie franchise we suddenly seem to be all starring in. It's time to count our blessings, look at the good things this time is doing for us all. For starters, we are for the first time in the history of the universe feeling like a truly collective entity. Like one gigantic—fruit.

In the BC (Before Corona) era, we were like individual slices of an orange. Tied together by superficial weak, woolly networks that were easy to break. But the AC (After Corona) era has changed all that. Now we're bound by this invisible virus that has us all tightly held together, like the *chhilka* of an unpeeled orange. So, you see, that's what the world has come to. A fresh, untouched Orange.

I tell my children that we're in this battle together, a collective unit beating the bad guys by staying home. Sita was told to do social distancing too you know, she was warned to not cross the *laxmanrekha,* but did she listen? And where did all her bravado and rebellion lead her, eh? So, we must listen to our dear Prime Minister, and believe in our collective past—good ALWAYS wins over evil. And we are good. We will be POSITIVE.

We did something super special yesterday. Celebrated thirty-six weeks in lockdown by hosting a party on Zoom with all our neighbours from the colony. Such a fun evening, the kids played virtual Name, Place, Animal, Thing and we all followed that up with with a good ol' round of Tambola. Even alcohol was allowed, I had mine in a steel glass though, it was a family event, na, even the oldies were online. I've told the kids to do a picture composition and write an essay on the evening they witnessed, when will they ever see something like this again? Why, it may even get picked for their school magazine, or maybe the newspapers would publish it? Later at night we had a grand feast—*alu tuk* with *alu paratha* and *alu rassedaar*. And Jayant did the dishes. What a feeling!

Oho, forgot to write about the best part of the evening. The dessert that never got made. Just as we were clambering into bed, Jayant thought we should round off the evening with a dessert. I agreed. *Gudh ki rotis* with *ghee*. Yumm. So at 1.25 am I started to knead more dough and the kids came in to help. Just imagine! Would you ever be able to do that on a regular school night? As I added more dry flour to my *atta*, the younger one tip-toed over. 'Can I do also, mama,' she asked in her sweetest voice. I conceded willingly—small joys of life—and the little one starts kneading the dough.

1.45 am, when would they get this chance again? She asks for a bit of dry *atta*, the older one being helpful passes her the entire box. She picks up a handful. Bits of the white powder escape her tightly clasped fists. Her hands are small. I bring out my *jhadu-kupdi*. The older one gets a naughty glint in his eye, he takes two fistfuls and flings them at the husband. The husband giggles childishly and returns the favour. I look around indulgently at all the white powder flying around, and as the powder begins to settle on my nose and eyelashes, the gas stove, the cutlery, the glasses, the newly washed utensils, the *katoris*, the floor, the sink, I stand transfixed. From the corner of my eye I see two tiny hands snatch the entire *atta dabba* from the husband and fling it high into the air. The seven-year-old in throes of delirium yells, 'Alexa!!! Play "I want to fly"!!' The husband and the offspring spring into action: '*IIII...want to flyyy like a rainbowww sooo highhh,*' they sing at the top of their lungs as they swirl around my freshly mopped floor which is now covered not just in a thick layer of *atta* but also their footprints. Jayant stretches out his hand, lovingly. '*Baad mein saaf kar lenge...kal kahin jaana thodi na hai.*' I drop the *jhadu* and leave the *kupdi*. And I dance. Not a care in the world. This is life. True life.

STATUS UPDATE

THUNDER RUMBLES IN THE DARK SKIES, THE RAIN lashes down, I jump out of my camper van—there's sludge all over the ground. In the distance another truck rumbles over—a faint medical sign can be seen on the tarmac behind it. It stops near the barricade with the rusting tin board that reads 'Quarantine Zone 1'. I pull my eyes away from the line of masked people with handcuffs being herded out of the truck towards the border that barricades 'US' from 'THEM'. On the other side of the border, men in hazmat suits wait anxiously.

Borders. Their definitions have changed since this thing began. I rush to the officer in army fatigues standing with some medical staff at a distance. His name badge is covered with splotches of mud but I know him by name. 'Colonel Saini?' He turns, his eyes register recognition.

He doesn't look happy. I don't care. I rush to him, pulling out my cell phone, 'Colonel, did you read it? Ridhi! My sister, she's still in there, her family too. Please, I beg of you. Get them out. *Pleeease.*' Tears of desperation roll down my face but he can't see them, it's raining too hard or maybe he chooses what he wants to see now. There's countless like me coming here daily.

He glances at me, he's a good man. I can see it in his eyes but even goodness has its borders. 'Sirji—*saare* positive *hain,* recheck *kar liya,*' calls the sentry from across the road, the colonel puts a tick next to the truck number on his clipboard. There's a page filled with numbers on it. '*Leh lo andar,*' he replies as he gestures for me to leave. I shake my head. It's a routine we follow, weekly. The soundtrack begins. A strange muted wailing. I'm used to it now. Humans are strange, you know; they do similar things when faced by similar circumstances. This could be a science experiment. Except it's not. Those are real people behind those masks, their mouths gagged, their hands cuffed. Certain that once they step across—there's no coming back for 'Them'. Not ever. If they survive, they'll be kept to work at the health department on the other side. This is their last plea. The muted wailing. It's always the same. Gulp. Focus.

His audio gets clearer, 'Ma'am I can't help, you know that already. This is a restricted area, civilians aren't allowed. Please don't make our job more difficult than it already is.' He starts to walk away, his gumboots splash water on my shoes. My feet get wet. I'll have to repair that hole again, once I get home. I hold his arm. Over-familiar. 'Did you read it?' I repeat. He pulls his arm away like he's been burned. 'What the hell do you think you're doing?' he hisses, nervously looking over his shoulder and then in a normal voice, 'Yes, I did, and they sound fine, ma'am. Happy, even. We're taking care of everything and we will get the healthy out soon. Now, if you'll excuse me.' He walks away.

I'm unable to control myself. The dam bursts. I scream, with all my might. I scream at all the lies and pretense. I scream for my sister and her world. I scream for the people being taken across the border. I scream at the information clampdown and the futility of the burning rage I have boiling within me. But the screams are in my head. In my reality I walk. I walk for my sister's tomorrow and for my parents who are waiting anxiously for me to return today. I walk away so I can fight tomorrow. I walk because I will find a way. I must.

In the distance the clouds rumble louder, I jump into my car. My eyes wander past the beaming smile of her profile picture and settle on her current status—'Bright sunny skies and the promise of a hot summer.' Liar. I hope to goodness they're okay. I drive away.

GREEN

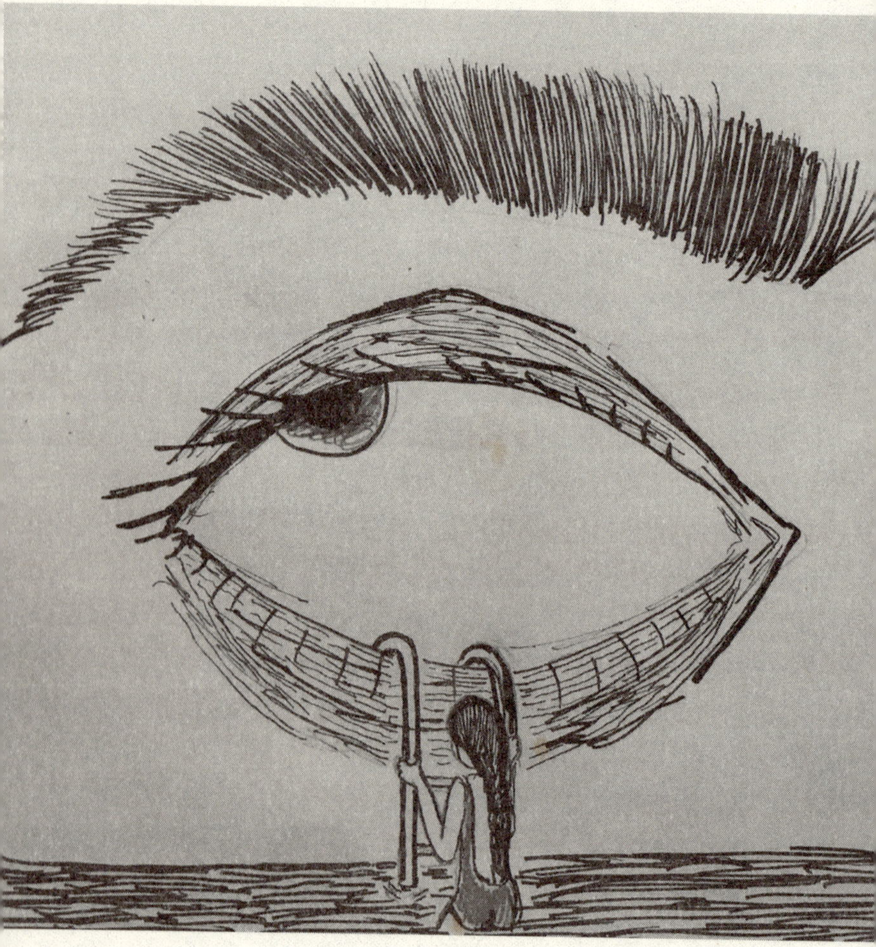

IT WASN'T THE NOISE THAT GOT TO ME THE DAY I forced the knife down his throat. I'd dealt with noise before. It wasn't the alcohol either. I'd been drunk before. No, it wasn't the white powder that still lined the membranes of my right nostril. Neither was it the girl in the green XS swimsuit who I'd caught him astride. It was the colour of her swimsuit—green.

After all, green was the colour of the tree of life. It was my colour—maternal, cooling, loving, giving. And so, I killed him. Just like that.

I'd chopped green beans with the same knife a couple of hours earlier. The kids love to eat beans and potatoes or maybe they don't—but it's healthy food and so I force them to eat it. Forcing—the word has many definitions, you know. Not all of them are negative. If I force the kids to finish their vegetables, I'm a good mom but if the PM forces me to live a life of his choosing, I along with all the liberals stand up in arms. I find this very strange about the intellectuals, the so-called left-leaning, including myself. Our entire view on life is convenient. It's privilege.

Privilege gives you the freedom to talk about choices. When you don't have food to eat or clothes to wear, you do as you're told to make ends meet. There's nothing called freedom of choice then, is there? Anyway, I digress.

So, I killed him, it wasn't as difficult as I'd thought actually, maybe because I'd just had all the knives sharpened by the sweet *bhaiyya* who goes past my kitchen window every other month. Maybe because I'd been contemplating this for weeks, carefully planning every micro second to the tee.

I'd dreamt of his eyes bulging as I carefully slit his neck with the precision of a surgeon which, incidentally, I am. So, it wasn't the cutting and the blood that disturbed me, it was just the general mess that we all suddenly found ourselves in, with my carelessly executed careful plan.

The young girl with the deep brown eyes and blood splattered over the green swimsuit stared at me in horror. Unblinking. She was petrified, naturally, being half naked—having me, Old Mother Hubbard with a bloodied knife in my hand hovering over her head couldn't have been a comforting sight!

I sighed, deeply appalled at letting my emotions get the better of me and walked across to the kitchen sink to wash the knife while I thought out this situation.

The girl in the green swimsuit was shaking uncontrollably now, in a half stutter, half stammer she managed a weak, 'Maydumji sowry, I was scared....*bhaiyya...bhaiyya bole* he would force me to leave the house. *Bahar toh hum kahan jaate*...I didn't know what to do.' She leaned against the wall and crumpled to the ground, crying helplessly. 'I'm sowry...sowry maydumji... sowry.' She reeked of fear and hopelessness as the poor often do and so I held my breath for a second. Things weren't ideal at the moment, but then the last six months had taught us a great deal about dealing with non-ideal realities.

I bent across the sink and peeked out of the kitchen window—below was the ambulance from the hospital waiting to take me back to work. There were innocents waiting to be taken care of. They needed me, lives that could yet be saved. And there wasn't enough time to deal with this. Not now at least.

'Laali, I'm heading in for a shower. Pack me a *dabba* with the *alu* beans I made this morning, I don't want to eat hospital food today. And pack me an overnight case.' From across the room the green swimsuit looked up, genuine horror in her eyes. 'MAYDUM JI BUT SIR?' she yelped.

I wiped the knife and set it back in the rack with the others. 'He won't be any trouble anymore. We'll deal with this day after, on my day off.'

Laali scrambled up, her butt cheeks peeking out of the swimsuit, her eyes searching desperately for her *salwar kameez*, her hands covering her non-existent bosom. I stared at her shamelessly, even enviously, for in that second as her eyes searched furtively for her clothes, she looked just like my baby girl Mira, when she used to step out of the club pool and with her eyes measure the shortest route to her towel.

My baby Mira who hadn't been back home for over six months, who I had bought this swimsuit for, last year from Zara.

But all pools had been closed down months ago, along with the parks and the malls and the cinema halls. No one went for a swim anymore. It was one of the many things that were now banned.

Like walking outside without a permit or driving a private car without a purpose or going to office unless you were part of the essential services brigade. Like I was.

'Tweeeeeeeennnn... Tweeeeiiiinnnnnn... tweeeiiinnnnnn'. In the silence the sound of the siren rang loud. The ambulance downstairs. It was waiting for me.

I picked up the discarded *salwar kameez* that lay brazenly atop the lone apple in the fruit basket and tossed it towards the green swimsuit. Baby pink with paisleys or are those lilies? Never mind.

The sound of the siren gets louder. My phone starts to buzz. I stride quickly towards my bedroom and just before shutting the door, I tell Laali to wash the swimsuit, fold it and put it back in Mira's drawer.

It used to be her favourite and when life goes back to normal and my baby comes back, perhaps she and

I could go for a swim again. Under the sunny skies, with her father sipping his ice-cold beer sitting by my side.

I sniffle.

RED

THERE'S A SOUND WHEN YOU SCRATCH THE NAIL OF your forefinger with your middle fingernail. A silent, disconcerting, itching sound Restless, impatient, unsatisfied That sound turns me on.

Our relationship began the day her nail polish started chipping. Chipping is perhaps not the right word, it was more a nasty peeling—neat but well-defined. Gel, not regular polish, that's what she used. Rashmi. The story of how we came together still sends shivers down my spine. If you'd met her, you'd know she was a connoisseur of 'good things'. And her impeccably kept glossy nails were a perfect reflection of her personality. Shapely, shiny, well-kept. And then her polish began its chipping peel, the glossy pink veneer giving way to a cracked, yellowing interior—that's when I truly started to notice her. The way her hair had started curling at its edges, the whites at the top of her head spreading, like a deadly uncontrollable virus, at breakneck speed, infesting her rowdy indisciplined mane that stubbornly refused to comply with any instruction. Like the bonny baby she was always clutching close to her chest. The one who never stopped crying—incessant, loud, unforgiving cries. Echoing. Endlessly.

I told her to try peeling off the gel completely, thought getting it off in one go might be easier than watching its slow disintegration. She was startled I think, to hear me speak, wasn't expecting it. But she gave my advice a shot, tried everything, from baking powder to boiling water before settling on her husband's favourite pair of scissors—the tiny ones he used to clip his beard. Suffice it to say, the scissor experiment didn't go as planned and the next time I saw her, she had big gaping wounds placed strategically just beside those peeling nails. So much for solutions. Strangely enough, she didn't blame me for what happened, kept away for a day or two, but returned soon enough. It seemed despite her initial hesitation, she was now beginning to enjoy our sessions together very much. I tried to dissuade her, multiple times, gently nudge her back to normalcy, tell her 'we' weren't possible. There was so much wrong with this equation—she was married, had a baby and was only in Maneshwar for a 'visit'. Didn't want to encourage anything that was difficult to sustain. My interventions though had quite the opposite effect. Instead of leaving me alone she started to visit even more often, sometimes more than a dozen times a day. The meetings that were earlier limited only to the night, once the caretakers had left, now started to spill into the day. She now stopped bringing in the baby, she brought in bottles instead.

Bottles that changed names with every day that passed. I asked her whether she was drinking without me too, but she denied it. I believed her, never had reason not to. She was a good person, kind-hearted and honest, from a well-heeled family of successful lawyers. Always in control and then suddenly not. I'm appalled at how it went south so suddenly, couldn't stop it from happening. There was no one there apart from me and the baby, by the time the caretakers came in the next day, it was too late. She was gone already and I'd left with her.

Okay, I admit, I indulged her too, but to give myself some credit it must be said that I'd tried keeping away from her for the longest. I mean, there's a reason ghosts haunt old, dilapidated, empty homes, and it ain't because we don't crave luxury or warmth. Believe you me, some of us are pretty rickety, having been around so long. Let's be honest here, who wouldn't enjoy lying on a soft comfy foam bed after a hard day's nothinging about? But peace does come first, where there's comfort there are people and with the people there is always chaos and noise. So, we stay away, most of us anyway. I'm different—found this sweet spot that I like haunting best. Holiday homes. Those are my game. A hell of a lot of comfort and a small compromise on peace, sporadically. I can deal with that. And so the weekend that Rashmi drove down here with her family, I folded myself into a small square the size of a baby kerchief and propped myself atop the cupboard in the guest bathroom (like I always do, to stay out of everyone's way). Unfortunately though this weekend didn't end like the others and when I floated down on Monday afternoon to reclaim my home, I saw Rashmi chilling on my favourite purple sofa with her impeccable nails in a teeny red negligee—the sniveller perched upon her chest.

It seems she'd decided to stay put for a few days, out of city limits until the situation outside settled down. She even convinced the husband to drive to the airport, drop the rest of the family so they could be on their way and return to the safe embrace of his wife and baby before nightfall. But he didn't make it back. Couldn't. A couple of villages along the way got sealed and Maneshwar was turned into a containment zone. I still haven't understood what exactly caused this pandemonium, doesn't matter really—what did, and still does is that we were now stuck together. Rashmi, me and that baby.

The helpers came in for a few days after, but then they stopped too. '*Jaan hai toh jahaan hai*', they were told. As the days turned into weeks, she started to look more like a ghost than me, barely getting any rest. Between getting the chores done and having the baby fed and slept, it was becoming impossible for her to handle. It was my suggestion to give the child a capful or two of whatever it was she'd been drinking, just to get it to sleep for a bit. She started taking it too far though, stopped bringing him along for our meetings, told me he was napping but I knew right away something wasn't right. I followed her that night, sat by her bedside while she rocked the baby, watched wordlessly as she walked him out into the verandah at one-thirty am, then three, then again at five am. Gasped, when she smacked his buttocks because he just wouldn't stop crying, stared agape as she held him out an inch, a teeny tiny inch beyond the edge of that parapet. She didn't let him go but I could see in the reflections of her deeply exhausted eyes, she could.

So, I found us a simple solution, told her she should try those scissors again, to get that polish off, I'd even help. She agreed quite readily. I held the scissors as she offered me her hands, hope glistening brightly in her eyes and I made them slip, the scissors, a teeny tiny bit, just over the edge of her fingernail, deep into the vein of her right wrist. I could see she was shocked. Hadn't expected it. Outside the baby began to cry as she stumbled towards the door. She hadn't realized yet that I'd already locked it. She would be stuck with me now, for eternity.

I stare at the life ebbing out of her, horrified with what I've done. But what else could I have done? Had to save the baby, didn't I? Then my eyes settle on her finger nails. They're coated in bright shiny red. They look glossy again. I start to smile.

Rashmi will be pleased. After all, my actions weren't for the baby alone.

SIYA, CIRCA 2020

Chips

SWEET COLD WINTRY SMILE. CHECK. STANDING IN MY social distancing circle. Check. My eyes firmly on the doorway. Check. Nose inside mask inside hoodie. Hand inside gloves inside jacket. Check. Four people allowed in at a time. I'm third in line, this may take a while. Air pods in. Ambience out. Check out.

This has been routine every two weeks since March 2020. People still need to eat. Essentials are still available and sometimes even luxury items. Ginger ale, dry yeast, pizza bases, why, you can even lay your hands on a can of baked beans, once in a while. It's getting the Blue Chips that still gives trouble. I'm not sure why, maybe because the Blue Chips factory was one of the first that closed down during the first lockdown, and it never reopened to full capacity. With most of their workers staying back in their villages, or whatever it is that's left of those. No one really knows what goes on beyond our own lanes anymore. Information is streamlined, vetted and controlled by the government and the health department. Dad says that's important, to stop the spread of panic. I agree. This has become the new normal.

No one talks to anyone in person, it's just not cool to do that. My best friend Raasha stays across the lane and sometimes we walk to the store together but we don't talk while we walk, tough having a chat with a mask covering your nose and mouth anyway. Mask-wearing is also no longer disconcerting, used to feel hot, sweaty, uncomfortable, but now it's part of your outdoor face. Me and Raasha made ourselves really fun, matching U2 ones with tees the parents bought us from that concert they went to, before concerts went virtual, that was. We got Bono on our lips, baby! Samaira has a pink mask with 'My Little Pony', made on it. Didi drew and painted it, as part of Sam's school project last month.

Anyway, Raasha didn't walk with me to the store today and that's a good thing because I can spot the last of the Blue Chips packets right on that shelf which means—'Excuse me'. I turn, my thought broken by the Voice. Dark brown eyes, jet black hair, the unmistakable 'Why So Serious' face mask. It's him. I feel my body stiffen. Is it the excitement of meeting him again? Can we call this a meeting? Okay, seeing. But I haven't really seen him, I mean, I have. But not really. Uhhh. Okay. Never mind. He leans across, a tad too close. Social Distancing Rule Break #1. I should move. But I don't. He picks up the last two Blue Chips packets on the aisle and notices I haven't moved, not an inch. 'Did you want them?' Chivalry in the time of Corona. Cute. I don't speak. Even my thoughts are staccato. He shakes his head, his eyes crinkle and he murmurs, 'I'll see you.' Did he just smile at me? And BOOM. He's gone. Sigh. '*Maydumji aage badhiye, aur bhi log hain dukaan mein*,' the shop-wallah *bhaiyya* calls out. I grab the Little Hearts packet and move.

'How do you know it's the same guy?' drawls Raasha as she paints her toes, a fuchsia pink with bright orange dots. *Ajeeb,* but she can carry it off. '*Arrey*, I can tell can't I? It was him! And…that nail colour isn't working,' I add, spitefully.

'Well then, you're lucky you won't have to see it, Mini Mouse! Just like you ain't getting to hang with Mr Masked Dark Knight Chip Thief, any time soon. How come you only meet him when I'm not with you? Maybe he's a stalker? Or some sleazy uncle?' she pipes. Truth be told I'm getting quite fed up of her know-it-all ways. She isn't right about everything, not anymore. I cut the call. Ooops! One of the positives of lockdown. There's nothing called polite conversations anymore. Sorry Ra...Bad network. Will connect later. Type. Send and Settle.

So, I'm not minding this whole lockdown business at all. It's worked out quite well for me. I wasn't very good in crowds anyway. Not much of a mixer, a bit socially awkward—you know the type? 'Middle of the rung.' Easily forgettable. Not spectacular at anything. One-of-the-many type. You know what I mean. Fact is, we weren't doing so well before the Virus came in. I mean, everyone was so busy being phenomenal that we, the 'non-phenoms', were quite frankly, feeling a bit left out. People going out all the time—parties, vacays, summer schools—the works! And then suddenly it was LIGHTS OUT. The 'phenoms' and the 'non-phenoms' part of one giant cosmos. Ginormous equalizer! Life redefined. In fact me and Raasha connected because of the lockdown and of course the Samriddh Colony App. Without those we belonged to different worlds. Any case, when you're searching for friends within a three-km radius you don't have many options, do you?

Which brings me to the most important thing. Finding people to date. Now, that's gotten tough these past couple of years. There's no way of meeting new people in the 'real' world anymore. Colleges have shut, most public areas have closed down or have very strict guidelines on the number of people allowed at a time. Areas are demarcated with chalk—four people per area, each standing in their own circle. There's a couple of coffee shops and restaurants still functioning. But you need to book your table days in advance. Each area has an app and you can book slots on things you want to do each day. Walks, Grocery, Runs, Restaurant Bookings, Coffee Dates, everything needs to be pre-planned and pre-booked. And everyone knows where everyone is going to be, because everyone needs to be kept a track of. Everything is on your colony app—quite simple really.

The slots for Recreation run out early so you need to be up at the crack of dawn every Monday if you're picky about what you want. There are ways of getting around the rules. Raasha, me and some boys from the neighbourhood have even snuck around a couple of times, pot and the like, but it isn't really easy. And getting caught is a nightmare. A Rule Violation stamp with a fourteen-day single-room quarantine. No exceptions. I've heard they're now putting public trackers on repeat offenders to ensure restricted movement. And they have drones patrolling most areas. The only way to keep out of trouble is to stay indoors. And that's where we stay most of the time—save my trips to the store which I must say I've started to enjoy tremendously. Especially since I've started 'bumping' into him. I smile. Wouldn't it be wonderful to find your one true love, at a time like this? After all, it's at times of great upheaval that the greatest love stories are born.

My fingers itch to reach for the laptop, I resist the urge.

'Siya, did you block evening walk slots for Di and me?' The Mothership. Drat! I knew I'd forgotten something. I fumble online, back on the Samriddh Colony app.

Scroll.

Scroll.

Scrollll—

Walk timings—Location.

Damn, everything's taken. Masjid Road 8.30 pm. Mom won't be pleased but it'd have to do.

Siya Mathur. Block.

Log out.

Okay. STOP. One last time wouldn't hurt. C'mon, it's godsent, I'm already on the app. I'll be careful. I start to type.

Novelty Super Mart.

6.30 pm. Blocked slots. VOILA. There he is.

Suparn Khanna, 32, Corporate Banker, 1025 Freedom Heights.

I click his profile for the forty-second time today.

Favourite buys—Blue Chips, Maggi, Amul Cheese.

Favourite Recreation—Back Road Running.

Ahhhh…That's new. Didn't know you enjoyed running, Suparn. What's your favoured time slot then? CLICK CLICK…BACKROAD…SCROLLLL…SCROLLLL… 6.15 AM! Hmmm…I've been thinking of becoming a Morning Person anyway. A little sun never hurt anyone! Whatsay?

Bachelor. Check. Lives alone. Check. Social Distancing Magnet. Check. Second chance meeting engineered right. Check. Now to fix the when and where of the third! I will see you soooon, Suparn Khanna.

So, Siya (2020) hang in there, you'll get here soon. And you will enjoy the Lockdown Life. Trust Me.

Xoxo

SIYA, CIRCA 2023

CYA

ABOVE: *AN EXCERPT FROM ONE OF THE LETTERS SIYA HAD supposedly been writing to herself.*

31 November 2023

The Freedom Heights Double Murders

MUMBAI: Last evening, the Mumbai police arrested seventeen-year-old resident of Andheri, Ms Siya Mathur, in connection with the Freedom Heights double murders. Siya Mathur, who lives alone with her mother, a former employee of the Blue Chips factory, is said to have been suffering from acute psychosis and schizophrenia for a while now. It is alleged that she was undergoing treatment for the same until the Lockdown of 2020 when her mother lost her job and her father, a senior manager on the now infamous 'My

Little Pony' cruise liner got stranded at sea along with his elder daughter and five-year-old granddaughter. They were one of the first few fatalities of the virus onboard the ship.

Sources claim the family has been under huge financial pressures and the mother has been unable to keep down a job ever since. 'The mother became a bit strange after the loss of her husband and elder daughter. We hardly ever saw her. Siya was a sweet girl though, a bit quiet but always helpful. We saw her walking down to the market every couple of weeks. Deeply shocked by what we are hearing,' says a neighbour.

The police have also recovered 'pages and pages of letters', that Siya was apparently writing to herself over the past couple of years. The last of these letters appear to chronicle her first few meetings with the victim, Suparn Khanna, who she apparently 'planned chance meetings' with at the local grocery store. This has brought sharp criticism against the government's new 'Aapki Colony App', which helps residents block time slots for their 'preferred' activities for the week.

The letters also bear mention of another girl from the neighbourhood, Ms Raasha Mallik, and claim Raasha was one of the offender's closest friends. 'Siya tried to connect with me on the colony app a number of times. But I always kept away. She was weird—asked me on chat one time about my nail colour. I got freaked out and blocked her. Didn't know her at all (sic)', says Raasha. She and her family are being taken for further questioning.

'We've found two cupboards filled with empty liquor bottles and packets with traces of marijuana in the house too. Yet to ascertain where the family was accessing these from. But we will get to the bottom of this. Anyone with information on the case is requested to come forward at the earliest,' says ACP Shinde.

Another neighbour on condition of anonymity claims to have heard strange noises emanating from the house in the dead of night, but refuses to divulge any further details. '*Ghar kitna ganda rakhtey the, main kya bataun. Chaar ghar chod ke bhi baas aati thi. Mujhe toh pata tha kuch na kuch toh chal raha hai vahan*'—(Their house was filthy, you could smell the stench from four houses away. I knew something horrible was going on there), he told this reporter.

The police are yet to establish the motive but suspect it is a case of 'jilted love'. Investigations underway. *More on pg 16.*

Murders Most Gruesome, pg 14.

Criticism for the Lockdown. What it's doing to our citizens, pg 16.

Family mourn for victims, Suparn Khanna and girlfriend Kiara Vaid, pg 16.

New mother from 'minority community' dies due to medical negligence, pg 13.

DEATH OF VIDEOCON

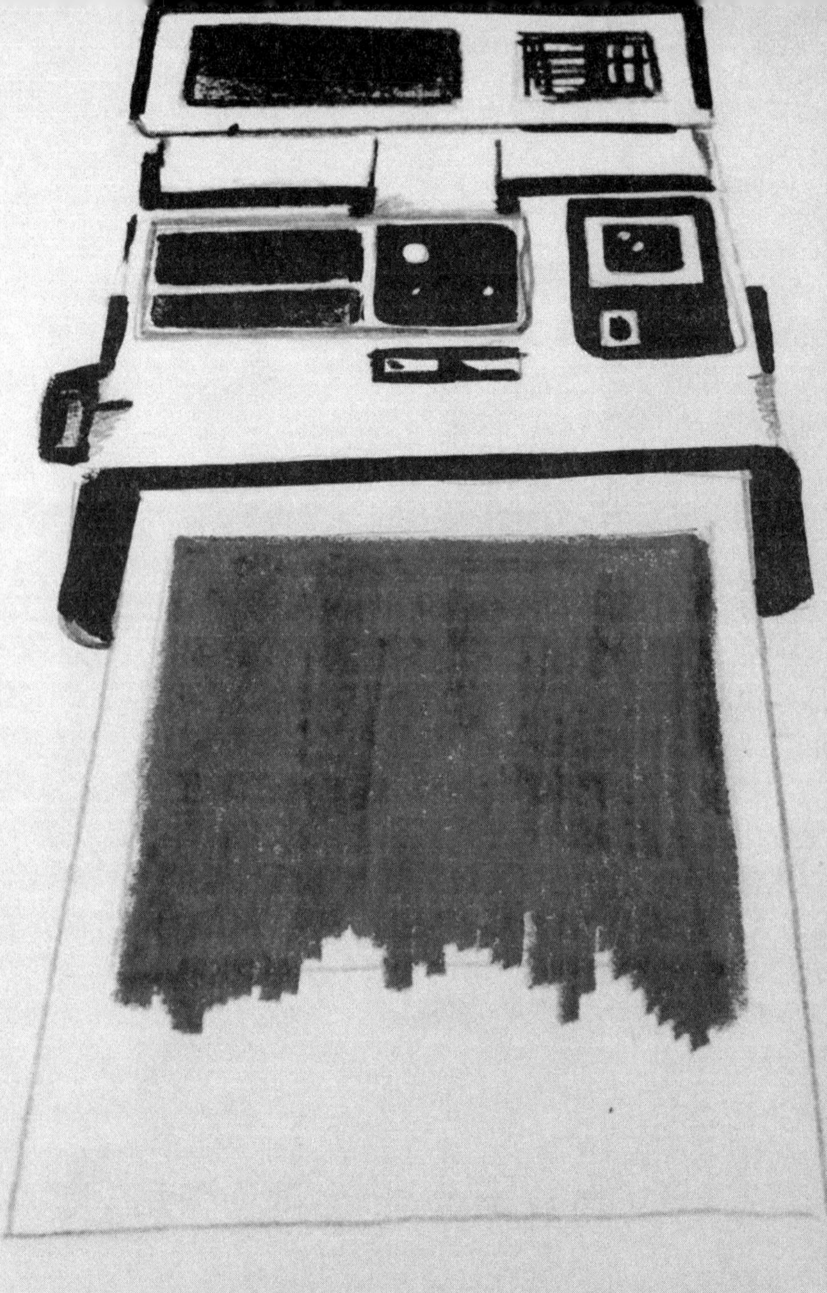

'...THAT'S WHEN I BEGAN SHOOTING HIM. OVER AND over again until there was no more of him left to shoot,' she drawled flicking her cigarette ash to the floor, her hair hanging carelessly over her eyes. 'So, then I began to hunk off pieces from his body—an elbow here, a finger there, why once I even chopped off a big chunk of his head!' she giggled. '...was easy for me to do, na? I'm a photographer, after all, it's what I do. Ya...so that's how it began. Boredom. I was bored.' She shrugged, a flirty challenging look in her eye as she stared directly into the frame. Inspector Damodar Venkatesh paused the screen and stared at the face that looked defiantly back at him. Intimidating. Overconfident. And devastatingly beautiful. The type of woman men thought of while they made love to their dull, compliant wives. The kind they dreamt of at night but would never take home to meet their mothers.

This was the beginning of her confessional statement and, yes, incredibly enough, boredom probably was the reason that this whole story began. The team that had investigated the case five years ago had found stacks of photographs of her husband, many with his body parts cut out of the frame. The husband wasn't dead in those pictures though, he was very much alive. Those pictures were, in fact, perfect 'family in lockdown' moments captured on film. Him laughing, playing with his little daughter, making pancakes in the kitchen. The only thing that made them creepy was the way bits and pieces of him were missing from all of them. Clicked by an amateur—or snipped off on purpose? Now Paroma Dhar, his wife and the person behind that lens, may have been many things, most of them of the awful kind, but being 'amateur' at anything was not her style. Especially when it came to composing faultless frames. She was an ad photographer, after all, known for her excellence on the job. What went wrong then? And why? Now that the original team had been taken off the job, it was Chief Inspector Damodar Venkatesh's lot to find out.

And there really wasn't a better man for the job. Known amidst his peers and seniors alike for specializing in finding 'missing' people, Inspector Damodar had spent the last five years concentrating solely on cases that occurred in the storm that had been the Covid-19 pandemic. For the eighteen months that the pandemic had ripped through the country, there were hundreds that went unaccounted for. People who just fell off the radar in the chaos of the months that followed that first lockdown, lost in the folds of time. Inspector Damodar had come across many peculiar cases from this time but this case he found particularly unsettling. A young woman was caught at the scene of a burglary at her own home and was brought to the police station for her statement. What was weird though was that after recording her statement confessing to her guilt, she had disappeared. Right from under everyone's noses. Poof! And she was gone. No one had seen or heard of her since, it was almost like she'd never existed. Inspector Damodar had been working the case for a week now—watching, reading, listening to everyone involved in the case and he still couldn't wrap his head around what had happened.

On the face of it, Paroma was a family woman, everyone who had known her claimed she'd doted on her husband, Amar, and their four-year-old daughter, Sameera. To all appearances, she'd led a charmed life and everything seemed to be going perfectly, until Demon Lover had crashed into them. Derailing everything like he'd been known to do before. Inspector Damodar was sure these dots were all connected and the answer to the riddle lay right here, in this recording of Paroma's confession. He just needed to concentrate and find the missing links. He scribbled on his notepad:

1. Who was Paroma Dhar?
2. What was going on in her mind when she spoke?

Then chewing the tip of his pencil, he hit the play button and settled in to listen to the rest of the recording.

'I got done with Videocon the day I took him for his MRI. I still remember sitting on that rickety plastic chair holding his mask, gloves and a small sanitizer spray when something inside me snapped. Suddenly I wished the ginormous MRI machine holding my husband's recumbent body in its womb would open its jaws and chew him up whole. Cut. Gnash. Slit. Snip him to shreds and spit him out. Then at least I'd be rid of him through no fault of my own. Once and for all he'd be gone. No such luck, though. Once the test got done, he gave me a thumbs up sign and the machine ground to a halt. An apt description of the marriage we were in, complete with its own soundtrack. The loud, techno, disturbing noise spewing from the machine's gut suited our current storyline quite well. I'd call it Electronic Bile. Come to think of it, may be that's how techno punk was invented. Perhaps some sweet acoustic guitarist went in for an innocent MRI and came out with a growth in his brain and a new tune. What do you think?' she asked, half giggling, much to the chagrin of the masked cop sitting in front.

Paroma referred to her family as a 'Videocon' family multiple times through the statement, it seemed to be her phrase for a picture-perfect universe. Like the flawless families that featured in all the TV ads, probably because that was the industry she was from? Inspector Damodar jotted down these points even as the policeman in the recording said curtly, 'Uhhh… ma'am if you could stick to the facts, please.' Damodar could see he was growing tired of her digressions.

'Sorry,' she mumbled, reaching out for her tea cup a tad too suddenly, her hand falling dangerously close to his. The cop sprung back, almost falling off his chair, face mask slipping out of place. Social distancing had still been a norm then. 'What are you doing?' he yelled. Angry.

She remained unfazed—this was obviously the reaction she'd desired. 'Oops! Sorry. Didn't realize…,' she shrugged swigging her tea casually, cup held in her cuffed hands like she hadn't a care in the world. Like she'd known all along that she would get away. But if she had wanted to escape, then why get caught at all?

The investigating team hadn't been able to get to the bottom of it. Fact was, this case hadn't been high priority, not at that time at least. There had been hundreds, no thousands, across the city being treated in hospitals, clinics, stadiums, racecourses, cinema halls, for the virus. The pandemic had been at its peak then and cops, doctors, municipality workers, everyone from the essential services brigade was stretched beyond imagination. A random robbery was the last thing on anybody's mind especially since it was discovered so easily and Paroma confessed to masterminding the plan so promptly. Broken her husband's heart, it had. He was a good bloke, still pining for his wife, Inspector Damodar had met him a few times. Barely spoke of her but had her hanging in happy frames all over their apartment. Five years since her disappearance and he still waited for her to return.

'…that was a Siemens machine,' Paroma droned on like she had all the time in the world. 'Does Videocon make MRI machines? I know Siemens does air conditioners, refrigerators and washing machines. They're also in the business of selling dreams but their advertisements aren't as good as Videocon's. I like their families the best….' Inspector Damodar sighed, fast-forwarding the tape now.

'I…know…*squaackk*…how to build…life… through its frames. *Squeeaaakkkk*…beautiful woman…brown curls…baby blue salwar kameez…*screeeechhh* with pearly whites…*scarrraaacchhhh*…dashing, supportive, super successful husband… *Squuuaaccccckkkkk* matching hues…by her side… beautiful children *squuaackkkkk*… stitched…order…*sccccrrrrrrrrrrreeee*…golden retriever *squuuoooooonnnnn*…perfect dog. I worked hard to make that family mine.'

Here it was, the most disconcerting part. Inspector Damodar leaned in, paper and pencil in hand, while Paroma continued her monologue. 'I made them into the most perfect little rounds so they fit nicely into all the right squares. Whittled away their edges and made them nice and smooth, all smelling sweetly of Comfort detergent. Both Amar and Sammy, I did that to. Even bought a golden Labrador to complete our family. But I had to give him away, he was too much work, that dog. Didn't manage to house train him. Amar was my most successful project yet. I worked hard on him, made him like Ken, Barbie's favourite doll. Clipped his wings and cut his chords, both vocal and umbilical, so he could fulfil my every dream. Just so. And then in that first phase of lockdown, I started to tire of his perfection. I'd always been a great believer in old world romance but when my love for him started to fade like the alphabets in a paperback left on a wet table near the pot too long, I think I started to lose my mind.'

Damodar left the recording on and walked to a side cabinet next to his desk to fix himself a drink. A rum and cola with a dash of chilly, just the way he liked it. He always kept a supply in the office, he never knew what time he'd get home, and god knew, he needed a drink after ten hours on the job. As he fixed his drink his eyes fell on his phone that had been charging on the cabinet all this while. Six missed calls from Sarita, three from Amma. Damn, he'd forgotten to tell them he'd miss the family reunion dinner. Sarita would understand, they'd been married almost twenty years. Amma he wasn't sure of. Anyway, he'd handle them tomorrow. For tonight belonged only to him and Paroma. He left the cellphone where it was and walked back to the couch with his drink. Paroma continued to talk.

'....the alphabets bleed, have you seen...slowly over the paper, leave black stains on the pages. The drops of water leave dirty brown splotches too. Water does that, you know, if it's left stagnant too long. It starts to rot. Gets infested by mosquitoes and worms and filth until there's no option left but to drain it. Now tell me, if water, the ultimate elixir of life, can turn into a black, stinky, lethal mass then a good solid marriage turning toxic should be par for the course, na? It's possible, right, for the problem between us to have been, that there was no problem at all, it was just...a natural progression of things?' she asked, this time quite earnestly, her eyes brimming with tears like she was truly seeking an answer. Inspector Damodar's eyes stayed transfixed on her as he chugged down his drink, and replayed some facts in his head.

He knew from the records and interviews that Amar was a gem of a guy. And it was probably this goodness of his, Damodar mused, that finally did her in. For Paroma had begun to loathe his every action. Detest his every move. She hated his smile when he brought her bed tea in the morning, felt nauseated by his constant selflessness, why, even the fact that he let her disappear into the dark room for hours on end without so much as a question irked her. It was like he had no opinion at all. A human form whose existence was irrelevant. He knew she had no work to do in the dark room, there were no films to develop, neither of them had been to office in months and hers had recently announced it would stay closed, until further notice. Yet he never questioned what she did in the dark room all that time. He was a software developer and had the option of going to office thrice a week, but had chosen to WFH for the entire year—to lend her a helping hand, he said. He'd been the one in their marriage who figured out all the logistics while she chased her dreams. But now his attempts at making her happy were failing miserably. In Paroma's cyanide-laced words, '...his sugary sweet *roohafza* love had started making me cringe. He didn't get me hot at night. Not even with porn. He'd always been morally averse to that kind of stuff, but I was beginning to change. I would watch porn on my iPad every night before coming to bed. But even that didn't help me get it on. We were together, you see. All. The Bloody. Time. And that MRI morning, just like that, Videocon stopped working and my love for the Videocon family was gone. I wanted suddenly to watch a more macabre tale—a child or two stuffed inside a washing machine, perhaps? I was so fucking bored. Pardon my French,' she chuckled wistfully. Inspector Damodar downed his glass.

Videocon, Siemens, Comfort, Barbie, Ken, all obvious references to the world she came from and the perfection she craved. A woman filled with insecurities, existing only for the superficial, suddenly got tired of it. She didn't want to do 'perfect' anymore and perhaps Kakia, the Grecian goddess of vices, heard her plea. For it was around this time (if the timeline etched out in the investigating officer's report was correct) that Paroma stumbled upon an old foe. A popular dating app she'd downloaded years ago as a dare in a heated argument with an ex-friend, popped up on her phone screen while she looked for a pussy cat feeding game for Sammy to play.

'Be Mine', the app in question, was a chart-topper that had a large and loyal fan base, yet Paroma had never logged into it, she'd always found the idea of seeking casual hook-ups quite disdainful, sleazy even especially if it happened in the virtual. However, in this brave new world of insanity, filth began to offer

Paroma a much-needed respite. She started to troll the dark alleys of the web now, knocking door to door, foraging for the forbidden. Everyone was home so the depraved world of the virtual was way more crowded than before but Paroma began enjoying her time there, jostling amongst all those degenerate lives. Stumbling and falling through this maze of the unknown, she now started deriving pleasure from perverted pain. Before she knew it, one casual dalliance with a single app turned into a full-fledged virtual orgy. And then there was no turning back. Kakia was the chat room name she gave herself, she'd been fascinated by her ever since she'd read about her in some novel. Occasional side chats with random men turned quickly into horny phone sessions that lasted many hours of every day. And then things got murkier still—video chats, lesbian dates, threesomes, S&M, there was no end to the stuff on offer. People were home, living vicariously in the virtual and Paroma was having the time of her life! While her little doll Sammy slept cuddled by her husband Ken's side, she travelled virtually into the darkest innards of human fantasy. Addicted, she became to her nightly fix, and then slowly her love for the muck started to infect her days.

Up until then her data records showed she'd been polygamous. Chatting hour upon hour with men and women of varied ages and multiple preferences. But midway through May 2020 something changed. That's when she met Demon Lover, 'The ying to my yang,' as she described him, 'the perfect answer to my prayers.' How he could be the answer to anyone's prayers, Damodar failed to understand, but then love is blind and Paroma's story was certainly a case in point!

'I met him on the dark web, in one of the many chat rooms I visited at the time. Been to so many, I've forgotten the name, doesn't matter, na? We got along, yes, but more than that I think it was the fact that he made me laugh. I began to feel alive again. Real. Like I'd been so busy living in the world of pretense perfection, that I'd forgotten how to breathe. Demon Lover became my breath of fresh air. I fell in love with him just talking. We didn't need any more than that to get us on. And then one day he suggested we meet.'

Her eyes moved nervously now side to side, her hand trembling slightly as she reached for her cup. Damodar noticed the golden band on her finger. 'Wedding ring?' he jotted in his notes while she sipped her tea (to compose herself?) and carried on, 'I agreed immediately, wanted to see the man I'd been talking to all these weeks. The fourth lockdown was on and there were partial ease-ups across the city. I told Amar

I needed some time out with my girls and drove off to Mullington Road that night. Demon had texted me his address earlier in the day but quite honestly, nothing had clicked. I mean, it had looked vaguely familiar but…anyhow the whole thing started to make sense the moment I entered his building. Clemency Towers. 64th floor.

'That's when I remembered. Clemency Towers had been in the news a few years back for a high-profile murder case. A man from an affluent background, a steel magnate, had strangled and then cut his sister-in-law into little pieces before stuffing her into a VIP suitcase and driving off to his farmhouse in Ratnawadi to bury her. He'd been jealous apparently of her growing proximity to a neighbourhood kid. People said his wife had been in on it too but no one really knew. Anyway, he got caught and convicted and the wife made off with his money. Shifted to his Parisian estate, she was in the news recently, in fact, did you watch? For tying the knot with her new toyboy, an ex-contestant of *International Survivor*. Quite dishy he is, *haan*? Check him out. Oho, I digress again, where was I? *Haan*, while she was having fun, her super powerful steel magnate husband, Jackie Khanna, rotted in jail. Two years he was here, I believe, wasn't able to get bail despite his swish influential friends. He was right here in Minar Jail, if I'm not wrong, but you know that already. Why you may even have met him a few times?' she asked, the flirtatious tone back. She was clearly in control again and definitely knew more about Jackie than she was letting on, but whether her rambling was deliberate or part of her persona, of that Damodar was unsure.

Paroma continued to talk, playing with a loose tendril now, seemingly lost in her tale. 'I was welcomed into the lobby with a puff of sanitizer spray and a new pair of gloves, then ushered into a private lift that was to open directly into his apartment. That's when the nerves hit, maybe because the lift was heading up sixty-four floors at jet set speed or maybe because in that one moment, I figured who I was about to meet. Demon Lover was *the* Jackie Khanna. Suddenly, so many things fell into place. Why he always wore masks through our chats? Why he loved to play "dress up"? Even why he liked me so much…I had a Lob—a long bob hair cut—much like the girl he had murdered. My blood ran cold, but now there was no turning back. I entered his home that night and never left. Until yesterday. And you know what happened next. *Chalo*, chat done.'

She grinned impishly, making to get out of her chair though she knew better than the cop in front of her, there was nowhere for her to go. 'Please ma'am, carry on,' he requested in a subservient tone, more aware than ever that the woman sitting before him was completely out of his league.

'Ok, if you insist,' she grinned. 'Never fancied myself as storyteller but apparently I do a pretty fine job, huh? Got you hooked! Anyway, now I'm getting a bit tired so I'll cut this short. I went in not knowing the guy I was about to meet was Jackie Khanna, but once I met him, I never wanted to leave. It seems you guys or your bosses in an effort to stop the spread of the virus in jails had taken a call to grant bail for first-time offenders from respectable backgrounds. And Jackie fell through that hole quite well, and it worked for us like a dream. Jackie was at home on bail and along the way we'd found each other. What more could two people want? When I didn't return that night, Amar wouldn't stop calling. I didn't call him back. I didn't miss him, nor Sammy either, I was in the throes of my Lockdown romance. We didn't step out of the apartment and no one came in. It was just us, cocooned in our most imperfect existence. I messaged Amar and told him I was fine but that I'd left him and was never coming back. He was sweet about it as always.

'Then Unlock 1.0 began and flight services started again. Jackie and me were worried that once the peak of the pandemic passed the authorities would come for him so we decided to make a run for it. Denmark is where we thought we'd go. Copenhagen, my most favourite place. He had some shady contacts and I clicked pretty mean pictures, as you know. So ya, we did a good job with his picture in disguise on a forged passport. Don't prosecute anyone for this, please. I mean there was chaos everywhere, everybody was in need of money. Organizing the passport hadn't been difficult and organizing the visa was easy enough too. Our problem wasn't the formalities, it was money. We needed hard cash to leave the country, to pay people off to get us out. All of Jackie's assets were frozen and if someone got so much as a whiff of what we were planning they'd have hauled his ass back to jail.

'That's when I had a brainwave. Robbing my house. It was my idea all along, Jackie was and is innocent of this, tried his best to dissuade me, but I knew it was the only way. After all, nothing could be easier, I knew all the codes to the safes, knew exactly where I kept my jewellery in the cupboard. We, uhhh, I planned this robbery down to the last detail. Uhhhhh…I need to go to the loo now,' she said mid story. The video stopped. Static.

Damodar rewound the tape and paused. There it was, the hand tremor again, she was upset at losing her lover, he was sure, he could see that clearly now. The story went that she and Jackie had entered her house late in the night when they were sure *Roohafza* Amar was asleep and snoring, dead to the world. He was an early-to-bed, early-to-rise type, went to bed at ten pm every night, and woke up at six-thirty. A sound sleeper too—not much could rouse him once he shut his eyes. The sleep of the innocent, Damodar thought wryly, that's what must have helped them out.

They accessed the safe, got her jewellery from her closet, but then something happened. She saw her daughter Sammy sleeping alone in her room, and it stopped her in her tracks. She told Jackie to take the loot and go, but he didn't, and they got into an argument. Now from here things got a bit blurry. A guard saw the two of them arguing from a window in the dead of night and alerted the cops. Jackie escaped with the cash and the jewellery, but Paroma got caught. End of story. Except it wasn't. A murderer on bail escaped the law and the woman who'd helped him disappeared two days after her arrest. The cops looked foolish and Amar was livid. For him his wife disappearing a second time was a double blow.

The media lapped it up, of course, the first sensational post Covid breaking news starring a steel magnate and a heartless vamp from the glitzy world of advertising. They couldn't have asked for more. The rumour mills went berserk. Some said Jackie came back to get her. Others claimed she got caught on purpose to buy him time to escape. The conspiracy theorists claimed the cops must've had a hand in her vanishing act, no doubt palms had been greased. No one was quite sure of the truth, but the fact was that Paroma had gone to the washroom accompanied by a lady constable and she had never come out.

Paroma had gone into the washroom alone and entered one of the stalls while the constable had waited outside. She hadn't gone in because the washroom that stank like a nightmare, now also looked like a sight from hell. There'd been some repair work going on before the virus struck, and the workmen had disappeared when the lockdown was declared, leaving behind sacks of debris and congealing tins of paint. Anyway the lady constable had waited outside patiently for a good fifteen minutes before she'd heard a crash coming from inside. A small slatted window in one of the stalls appeared to have been broken but there was no way a human could have slipped out from there. It was barely big enough for a monkey.

From here all hell broke loose. The cops, the jail personnel, every person in fact save the prisoners in their cells, had searched high and low, but Paroma had vanished into thin air. It had been about five years since the incident, and there was still no trace of her. Jackie, though, had surfaced a couple of years ago at a London party, hobnobbing with his ex wife. It seems he had managed to pull some favours, grease some palms with Paroma's money, and got himself on a flight with the forged passport and visa. Gone to England, not Denmark, like Paroma had planned. By the time the authorities found out, the prodigal pigeon had flown the coop.

A couple of days ago Inspector Damodar had managed to get on an offline chat with Jackie via some of his sources. But he claimed to know nothing of Paroma's whereabouts, something he had stuck to over the years. He'd mentioned instead the email he had written to Amar a little over a year ago, expressing his profound grief at having lost the love of his life. Jackie believed there was more to Paroma's disappearance than met the eye and urged Amar to find out more.

All this was on record already, Amar had reported this email in the past. Another blind lead? Inspector Damodar sighed, glancing at his watch as he went through his notes once more. Ten pm. Too late to call? Too bad. He dialled.

'Good evening, Inspector. Any news?' asked Amar, taking the call at the first ring like he always did. As if he sat by his phone all day waiting for someone to call with news about his beloved. Inspector Damodar felt a twinge of guilt every time he spoke to him, wishing he had something to tell him, but he didn't. 'Uhhh, hi sir. No sorry, no news, just a couple of things I wanted to discuss with you. About that last day at the police station. You were here, right, while she went in to give her statement? Could you come to the station tomorrow morning? Eleven am or so?'

'Of course,' replied Amar evenly, 'I'll be there.' A moment's pause. 'You know, Inspector, it's been 1,875 days since Paroma went missing and I still find it impossible to function without her, in fact without her I can barely breathe, exactly like it was the first time she left.'

Inspector Damodar let out a deep breath. 'What a good, good man,' he thought. 'Why would any woman in her right senses leave him for that creep? Strange are the minds of men or women, as the case may be. Truly.' Aloud though he kept it official. 'Yes, sir, we will do our best, I promise. Hope your daughter is well. Sorry for disturbing you so late. Goodnight.'

Amar put the phone back in his pocket as he continued his walk towards the new kids play area in the grounds of his apartment complex. He along with the other residents of the housing society had contributed towards building it. Just a few weeks ago, they had decided to dedicate it to the memory of those they had lost to the pandemic. There had been a small ceremony, presided over by the president of the RWA, and they had unveiled a plaque with all the names of those who had lost their lives. Paroma's was one of them—though of course, no one knew for sure if she was dead or alive. He sat down on his haunches as he did every night and touched the engraving of her name. *Paroma Dhar*.

Where these beautiful swings, slides and merry-go-rounds stood today, there had once been a gorgeous, Olympic-sized swimming pool. Where, not so long ago he, Sammy and Paroma had spent many a lazy Sunday afternoon. But swimming pools had been the first to be banned when the lockdown was declared, and continued to be so even when Unlock 1.0 began. When, after the first lockdown, the stagnant water in the pool had turned brown and stinky, the RWA had the pool drained, and it had lain empty for many months. Amar had been the one to propose that they fill it in and turn it into a playground for the kids, and everyone had supported the idea. Once the lockdown was lifted, and construction work could resume, they had put the plan into action.

Amar touched the smooth edge of the cool gold wedding band, the only thing of hers he'd kept. He pushed open the gate of the play area and walked slowly inside. Then he sat on the small merry-go-round and touched the ground beneath it. That's where she lay now. Beautiful as she had been in life, and his to have and to keep. For the first time.

Amar hadn't lied to the Inspector. Just told him a half-truth. He truly couldn't breathe when Paroma wasn't around so he'd found her the perfect resting spot. One that she could not escape, that would keep her with him forever. She would've appreciated the poetic justice he thought, lying here silently while all those noisy chaotic Videocon families with their children trampled upon her day after day, month after month, year upon year. Her body crawling with anger and disgust at being locked up, except this time there was no getting out.

The Inspector was right. He had been at the police station the day she'd given her statement. He hadn't heard what she'd said, of course, he'd sat in the corridor outside but she'd told him everything before the cops arrested her, right after Jackie left. And he had told her he'd help her get out, reunite her with the man she loved. He loved her enough to do that, and she knew that. She was his creator, after all. He always handled the logistics so she could achieve her goal. So he made a foolproof plan whose audacity lay in its simplicity. Small simple commands fitted in just so, like pieces in a virtual puzzle where you pressed GO and everything just CLICKED into place. Much like the software programs he designed for a living.

He'd noticed the debris lying around the jail washrooms on his visit there the very first day. Had noted the quality and colour of the large gunny bags filled with rubble lying piled up in the corner of the women's washroom. He heard and recorded in his mind the cops talking to each other about how the admin officer had been calling the contractor for days, to send his labour to clear the debris, but he said none of his men had returned from their villages. All of this he used as a base to build the most perfect plan. The perfect set of dominoes he placed so everything would fall just so.

That morning when Paroma was led into the interrogation room from her cell, he was waiting for her in the corridor. He rushed to her and hugged her– no one had stopped him—a poor victimized grief-stricken husband professing love for his cold-hearted bitch of a wife. What they hadn't seen though was that while hugging her he'd slipped a small note into her palm and whispered into her ear that the route to her escape lay in the loo. She needed only to follow his plan to the tee.

Then he'd sat outside counting the minutes while he waited for her to excuse herself to go to the washroom. He knew she must be rambling on with her story, as she often did whilst she made up her mind. When she stepped out accompanied by the lady cop he watched her with a silent calm. She'd made her decision, he knew.

She did as he had instructed in his note. Went into the washroom, saw the many gunny bags filled with debris lying by the side and also the empty one he had placed there, just for her. She pulled it into a corner and picked up a large stone. She threw it at the window with all her might before climbing into the sack and pulling it over her head. The glass of the window shattered to the floor while she lay silently in her sack and just stayed still.

Outside, there was pandemonium. The lady cop rushed into the washroom and checked all the stalls. She rushed out screaming that Paroma was gone. A possé of cops swarmed into the washroom and searched the stalls again. That's when their gaze fell on the slatted window with its mouth agape. No human, not even a child, could squeeze through those slats and yet the mind of man grows foolish in the face of the impossible. It can be made to believe anything if played with just right. They ran helter-skelter looking for her and yet no one looked in the most obvious spot. Searched everywhere when the whole time she had been lying right there. For six straight hours they searched while Amar raised quite a stink himself. Watching and waiting for the right moment to execute the next part of his plan, he'd watched enough movies with escapes of this kind. Movies with a lot of blood and gore, the type Paroma had grown to love in Lockdown 4.0. It was from one such particularly gruesome movie that he'd drawn inspiration for Part Two of his plan.

While the cops and the jail authorities went into panic mode, a turbaned, bearded labourer in a dirty banyan and checked lungi entered the police station and went up to the admin officer. 'Contractor *saab ne bheja hain, woh samaan ko uthane*,' he said.

'Kahan mar gaye the, saale, kitni baar phone kiya tumahre contractor ko,' the officer growled.

'Kya karein saab, kal hi tho aaye gaon se. Aur contractor *saab ne seedha yahin bheja.* Police *ka kaam* priority *hain, unho ne kahan.'* The harried officer grunted and waved him in the direction of the washroom.

The labourer lifted a couple of sacks on his shoulders and took them out of the station. Then he returned for a third one. In all the chaos, no one noticed that he didn't come back.

Once outside the station, Amar walked with the sack on his shoulder to a quiet side lane round the corner. His blue Mercedes was parked there. Looking up and down the road to make sure no one was around, he slid into the front seat and quickly divested himself of his disguise. He rolled it into a ball and threw it into the bushes, and pulled on his shirt and trousers. Then he swung the sack into the boot of the Mercedes and drove off.

He continued to drive until he found a silent stretch of road. Then he drew up and opened the boot, and let her out of the sack. She was dishevelled and red in the face with the effort of breathing, but alive. He still remembered how she had hugged him and cried, told him how sorry she was. 'You're too good, Amar,' she said, '...too good for me. I'm sorry. I don't deserve you. Where's Jackie? Can I call him?'

He'd kept his cool, didn't want her getting suspicious. He handed her his phone and just as she began to dial, he bludgeoned her from the back. A big thwack on the back of her head with one of the bricks from the jail. She crumpled to the ground, a wide-eyed look of surprise on her face but she was still breathing, he made sure he didn't hit her hard enough to kill her. This wasn't the moment. He lifted her and put her back in the boot along with the stone. Gagged her and tied her hands too, with her favourite pink flamingo scarf, he really had thought of everything. Then he drove back to the parking lot in their apartment complex.

At three am that night, when all was still, he went down to the car. Made sure none of the guards were about, then took her out and marched her to the pool.

Work on the pool had begun the day before, and the labourers had filled it to the brim with cement. The cement was still wet, and they would have to wait till it hardened before they could start converting it into a playground. Just yesterday, a couple of kids playing nearby had dropped their cricket ball into the pool, and it had been swallowed up by the cement. They had stood by and watched it disappear, the cement closing over it. That's what gave Amar the idea for Part Three of his plan.

She went down without a whimper with that big stone tied to her calf. Her hands tied with the flamingo scarf, he could see she noticed it as she went down, perhaps even had a glint of pride in her eyes, before her body got swallowed up by the wet grey cement that had once been their sunshine pool.

Maybe she was happy, that just as he had been her Ken once, he could also be her Clyde.

You know what was strange? Bonnie had been a photographer too.

As he walked away, Amar began to hum 'The Ballad of Bonnie and Clyde', one of her favourite songs before she left him the first time.

Bonnie and Clyde were pretty good-looking people
But I can tell you people
They were the devil's children…
Bonnie and Clyde began their evil doing…
laalaaalaaaa

A week later, when the cement had dried, the labourers returned to complete the job. They brought machines to smoothen out all the uneven patches in the cement, and turn it into a happy playground where innocent children could run about and laugh and play.

He was Paroma's Perfect Ken after all. And he knew how to get things done right. She'd made him like that. Perfect for everything, even for committing the perfect crime.

He smiled now as he put the ring back into his pocket and started to walk back home. It was getting late and Sammy was all alone. He would meet Inspector Damodar again. Tomorrow.

As he walked, Paroma's gold ring rolled out of his pocket and settled under the merry-go-round. It glinted now in the moon, waiting for one of the Videocon families to spot it. Tomorrow.

MUMMYJI AND PAMMI

HE AND THE *CHIPKALI* CRAWLED OUT OF THE ROOM together. Mummyji got her son back, and Pammi secured her chance at playing Mummyji someday. That's why the elders always proclaimed that Mummyjis were far superior to Mummys. It was true. Whereas Pammi's biological Mummy would have just sat and snivelled, too scared to take a stand, her Mummyji seized the moment and became her partner in crime. What's more, they got rid of the biggest pest in the Bhandari household without spending a rupee. Their respective husbands would've been proud of them, had they been there to see.

As they sit now in their garden with the gloriously flowering bougainvillea, Mrs Bhandari and her daughter-in-law, Pammi, sipping their evening *adrak* chai, munching on Marie biscuits, they sigh as they watch their cherubic sons play softball on all fours. Yes, things had worked out just fine, once they had let their masks drop. Now their organic veggies business was booming and the flowers were doing all right too. To think they had started on this journey only eight months ago. If I have to put a finger on it, I'd say their luck turned the day he smashed Pammi's head on the bathroom mirror.

She had split that day into a hundred pieces reflecting in fragments of mirror that scattered across the cold hard floor. Each piece promising its own seven years of ill luck. It was only an illusion, of course, for in the flesh Pammi wasn't broken, she lay sprawled across the toilet seat. Shattered, bleeding, broken they lay, both Pammi and his beloved commode. For as she fell, she had grabbed the flush tank for support, and it had come off the wall with a crash, taking Pammi down with it. Now the commode's illicit relationship with the sewage pipe lay exposed; a big spurt of water from the pot's behind sprayed across his face. The commode at least had reacted violently to the abuse. All Pammi and Mummyji had only ever done was cry.

This wasn't the first time he had hit her and both Mummyji and she knew it would not be the last. But it got worse once he lost his toilet, his one safe spot in the house. Maybe it was because the commode and its attachment, the sewage pipe, had silently borne witness to so many of his vile desires for so long. Now deprived of his usual outlet, unable to seek any other until the lockdown lifted, he vented all his ire on Pammi. He became a raging bull around the house, not even needing an excuse to punch or pummel her .

He made Mummyji dial the plumber even before she called the family physician. Both said the same thing—they were not available for home visits, not until the lockdown eased. By the grace of *Waheguruji*, Mummyji was good at first aid and had in her possession a large box filled with medicines of every kind. Like the small suitcase that Mary Poppins carried with remedies for every need under the sun, this battered blue tin box too held medical bits and bobs. Bottles filled with pink and green syrup, swabs, bandages and Band-aids. Painkillers to take away the deepest aches and pains. And pills that could keep you dreaming sweet even on the most nightmarish of nights. Mummyji had lived a full life, no one knew better than her that it was up to the women of the house to always be prepared. No matter how big or small the calamity, finding solutions was what women were born for. So she took care of Pammi. Patched her up perfectly well. It was the commode that had suffered more damage, it was beyond repair.

Her son was livid now at what the 'fat cow Pammi' had done, he really wanted to 'give her another one' and when Mummyji intervened, for the very first time in her life, he returned the favour by kicking her in the gut. This was a first for him too. He'd never hit out at his mother before. But he'd lost his mask of 'respectability' that day in the toilet and both Pammi and Mummyji knew this was something he may never find again. From the way things were unfolding now it seemed he wouldn't even try.

Starting from that day, they began using the tin box every single day. Like cocaine addicts who could never get their fill, the ladies of the Bhandari house used the contents of the magical medicine box. For there wasn't a day since that 'gut-kick' morning that he had not raised his hand on them.

Until the day came when they'd had enough and they just locked him in. Into the room with the damaged WC. He wasn't the only one who had lost his mask, the masks the ladies of the house wore were slowly slipping too. Everyone looked uglier in lockdown—straggly eyebrows, split ends showing, no one bothered with make-up anymore. Why, some women had even dispensed with the support of their bras in the endless round of household chores. And it wasn't just the Bhandari family that seemed to be unravelling, looked like the house was in the process of letting go too. The pests had started crawling out—cockroaches, *chipkalis,* rats, lizards—creatures of the night all having a field day while the pest control guys stayed away. Like the beautiful picture of Dorian Grey, the outer facade of the entire Bhandari household was slowly being replaced by who they truly were. Turns out their home was quite a hotspot of horror, they just hadn't realized it before.

Pammi's husband now began to use the loo that led off from the sitting room, the one usually reserved for guests. Except there were no guests anymore, so he had it all to himself. He would sit inside for hours smoking cigarettes and blowing out toxic fumes of death. Fumes that would snake out and make their way to Mummyji's vintage windpipe and the placenta in Pammi's womb. Did I mention that Pammi had been pregnant all this while? Six months of life she had already built within. That's what drove Mummyji to it, I think, she would never have stood up for Pammi if she hadn't been carrying the heir to the Bhandari family fortunes in her womb.

Whatever the reason, one Sunday afternoon when he'd finished his last pack of cigarettes and was getting ready to light into Pammi again, she went up to her son and said, 'Lay off. Go. Get out.' As simply as that.

He didn't listen to her, no surprises there—he tried kicking her again instead. That's when Pammi's mask, already loosened at the hinges, fell off. From her face, mutilated with all those cuts, scars and marks, a surge of power emerged. She wrenched herself free from his grasp and smacked him hard across the face. Her wedding ring hit his eye and he roared in pain. Swore he would finish her off that day. He picked up the steel-handled mop that was propped against the bathroom wall and rushed at her.

Then something extraordinary happened. Mummyji came up from behind and jumped on him piggy-back. Her saree rode up to reveal two knobbly knees that even Pammi had never seen. She grabbed his hair and punched him sharply in his ribs. When he doubled up in pain, she said, 'This is something I should have done years ago.'

Yes, maybe she should have hit him when she saw Pammi emerge from their room with those dark blue splotches across her chest last year. Or perhaps the year before when she'd watched in silence as Pammi sobbed in her bedroom, trying to wash the writing off the wall with her blood. All these years Mummyji had kept quiet and Pammi had tried to cover up her bruises. Sure, it had got worse during the lockdown but, Mummyji now realized, she should have nipped it in the bud when it began. Turned him out of the house, called the neighbours, the police, if need be, anything to stop her daughter-in-law's suffering. For Mummyjis had been Mummys too, once.

He didn't give up even then and came headlong now straight for her. That's when Pammi took the iron kadhai filled to the brim with hot dal and crashed it on her husband's head. She stepped back in shock and watched as he finally crumpled to the floor. Lifeless. Almost. Now both ladies of the respectable Bhandari home stood without their masks for the very first time. They sized each other up as they summed up the damage, both unsure now of what to do next, petrified of what he would do once he came round.

That's when they saw the *chipkali* emerge from his room—the master bedroom he shared with Pammi—and an idea most preposterous came to Mummyji's mind. She looked at Pammi and knew the same thought was forming in her mind too. So together they dragged him to the room and lifted him onto the kingsize bed. Gently now they placed him upon the white satin bedspread and from the magic medicine box Mummyji tended to the wound on his head. She bandaged it and gave him some pink syrup for the pain. Then they left the room and locked the door behind them.

That's where he stayed for the next five months, in the room with the damaged bathroom, the bathroom that held his beloved commode. While the Pandemic raged outside, they kept their monster reigned in. For the first few days, he screamed and shouted and cursed, but they didn't relent. Then the medicines from Mummyji's medicine box took over, and he grew quiet, sleeping mostly. Until then, it was tough for Mummyji to hear her *laadla* cry every night, but Pammi held her hand all through, just as Mummyji held her down when she gave birth to her firstborn.

Pammi had shifted into Mummyji's bedroom for these last few months and together mother and daughter-in-law had tended to both their sons. For the elder, they left food laced with sleep-inducing medicine and Mummyji cared for him lovingly in this sedated state. She bathed him and cleaned him, why, she even shaved his beard! And she put adult diapers on him, so he wouldn't soil the sheets. She sighed as she changed him, thinking of his baby days. In that time, the Bhandari ladies had got tech-savvy and ordered all their supplies online. They used Amazon for deliveries and along with their groceries, they ordered diapers too—one lot for newborns, and the other for adults.

The ladies were not happy with what they'd done but in their heart of hearts they knew that if they had let him out, there was no saying when he'd revert to type again. And now they had a new Baby Bhandari to watch out for. So they kept him locked in the master bedroom throughout the four lockdowns, and a couple of the Unlock terms too. Completely isolated he lived and the Bhandari women kept silent, not breathing a word of what they had done.

That's how the Bhandaris survived the Covid Pandemic. And when they finally brought him out, after all those months of solitary confinement, they realized that he had gone a bit cuckoo. Like he'd gone back in time, regressed to being a two-year-old. Solitary confinement could do that, Pammi had read on the Net, and the constant sedation had probably had an effect too. He'd become child-like, innocent. The perfect son Mummyji had never had, made a great playmate for his son too.

Like I said, it all worked out quite fine in the end. Mummyji got her wayward son back, and Pammi got a shot at playing Mummyji too. Someday. For the first time in years, the Bhandaris all shared a cheery camaraderie, and all four of them lived happily ever after.

INFECTION

THE STATE OF THE STATE MUMBAI
WEDNESDAY 29TH APRIL 2020

STATE OF TH

SoS City (Contd.)

'Minority' mother dies due to medical negligence

Turned away from hospitals

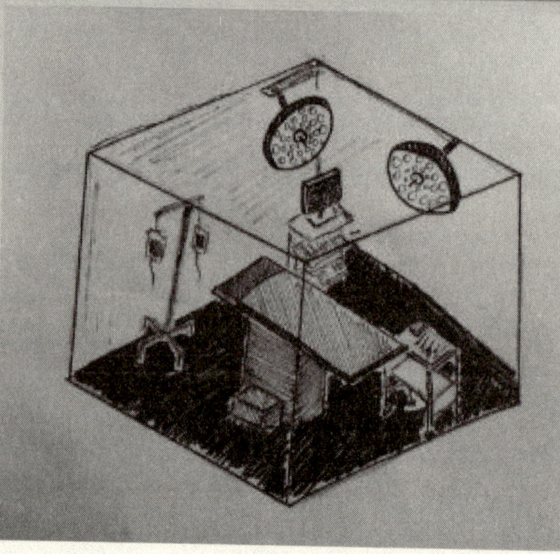

iMumbai, 30 April– Into the OT – she never did get to meet her baby. Not really. And that, ladies and gentlemen, is the true story of Azaan's birth, She would've taken it to her grave but since that's where she was resting now (I hope, since that was a whole story in itself), she thinks it's okay to share it. This whole 'birthing process' wasn't really a walk in the park, if you know what she means. Far from it. She agreed the circumstances surrounding them weren't ideal but

YOU'RE IN THE THEATRE. YOUR DEBUT PERFORMANCE. Excited. The lights blinding. Air conditioning turned up high, too high—goosebumps. Your heart beats faster as more and more people join in. You lie there—centre stage—breathless with excitement. And suddenly the curtains come down. You can't see beyond your waist now. You're nervous, scared, petrified. You want to jump, run, hide. But you can't, you're strapped in. 'Breathe madam, today's going to be the best day of your life,' says the blurry doctor with the mask on his face peering between your legs. The rest of the crowd gets into action, a small needle prick, the nurse beside you holds your hand tight. A chorus of voices now—'Deep breath and relaxxxx... Breeeeathe...Deeeppppp.'

Wish I'd known then, how much I would miss this deep breath, the one that comes from the deepest deep crevasse of your lungs. And, I wish they had allowed me to take my spectacles into the OT—I never did get to meet my baby. Not really.

And that, ladies and gentlemen, is the true story of Azaan's birth, I would've taken it to my grave but since that's where I'm resting now (I hope, since that was a whole story in itself), I think it's okay to share it. This whole 'birthing process' wasn't really a walk in the park, if you know what I mean. Far from it. I agree the circumstances surrounding us weren't ideal but even in the best of times, 'birthing' wouldn't be my go-to activity. Strangely, though, it wasn't the delivery process or what happened before it that killed me. It's what happened immediately after.

In February this year, when the riots broke out in the city, Ammi, Abba and the rest of my family lost their home. They heard about the attacks before most others because my brother-in-law, Bilal, works as a ward boy at Bhabha National Hospital. He heard of the ambulances being dispatched to Kardampuri and gave them a heads-up. Good thing that, because their house got razed to the ground. Burnt, people say, but no one's quite sure, there was so much going on that day. I mean, even the school where the kids studied wasn't spared. Ravaged. The family came to us, but only for a few days. There were eight of them and four of us with another on his way. The house was cramped and I already had the older boys and Jameel to look after. They didn't want to stress me out, I think. So they left for Aurangabad, our family home. Bilal wanted to go too but he couldn't get leave from work, so he stayed back while the others decided to return only when things were resolved. And it was decided that Ammi would settle the family and come back closer to my delivery date, I would need the help. I'd never done this before. But things never did get resolved and Ammi never came back. Newer things came up instead.

To tell you the truth, our area stayed pretty unaffected by the trouble. People kind of stuck together and didn't let the outsiders in. We stayed safe, but the stories of what everyone else went through were quite devastating. Much like what happened later. Anyway, in the first week of March, a big prayer meeting was called to commiserate with the people who had lost their near and dear ones in the trouble. Now, neither me nor Jameel are particularly political, but this was different, it was about solidarity. Jameel wanted the older two (his kids from his previous marriage), to feel part of the community, so it was decided we would attend. On the day of the event, however, I opted out. The baby was growing bigger by the day and it was getting tougher for me to breathe, let alone get around. The doctors had told me to take it easy, I could go into labour anytime. So Jameel took the boys and Bilal joined them. Later, he joined us for dinner. I'd made *sheer khurma*, which we ate while Bilal told us of the horrors he was witnessing at the hospital. He felt things were headed for a change, the nationwide uproar, candlelight marches and *dharnas*, talks of the government being held accountable. I don't know how much of what he was saying was true, how much of it happened or is still happening. What I do know is, that Bilal was the last person I met before my lungs gave way. He even brought me the 'magical' hydroxychloroquine tablets, hidden in his uniform. The medicine didn't help. I'd never needed it. But no one tested me, so they never knew.

I don't blame them, you know, they were hard-pressed for time. This was an emergency no one had anticipated. Delivering a baby amidst this crisis must've been taking its toll on them too. And then I started to show symptoms of their biggest nightmare, right there in their recovery room. The news reports playing out at the time didn't help my cause. Nor did the fact that Jameel was truthful about the prayer meeting he'd attended. So they believed the worst. Maybe 'fear' as an emotion needs a face, it needs to physically manifest into an object or a person. It needs tangibility to exist for you to fight it. And at a time when the one thing the whole world was fearing was invisible, perhaps having 'someone' to blame was the most natural reaction. So they did what came most naturally to them—quarantined everyone who'd been part of my performance earlier in the day and told Jameel they would need to discharge me. 'We aren't equipped to deal with the illness your wife has. It requires different care, you must take her to one of the special hospitals,' they said. Jameel tried his best to reason with them, tell them I'd been home for almost a month. Even explained we weren't part of the big congregation that everyone was referring to in the news reports. We weren't part of the sect they were talking of. But the face of fear, ruthless, dark and deeply unforgiving, made them deaf. They discharged us—me and my baby. 'He may already have the virus, don't want him infecting the others.'

Jameel tried his best to get me help, took me to over ten hospitals. But, no one took me in. Not even the 'specially assigned' ones. Maybe they were full up or maybe I looked like I wouldn't make it anyway or perhaps they were scared of getting 'infected' too. He tried to take me back home, but the neighbours refused to let us in either. Bilal came while I waited in the auto for Jameel to figure what we should do next.

Azaan was born healthy. 2.8 kg. Caesarean. No complications.

They tested me after I was dead, to check if I had been infectious.

The test was Negative.

Cause of Death on my certificate read 'Acute Respiratory Distress Syndrome (ARDS) post Delivery.'

Someone wrote a news piece about me, which featured on page 13 of the paper, and all was forgotten.

But I was horrified. They sent my child home without treatment. He was already infectious. I'd infected him at birth with the disease that killed me. The one that me, his father and countless others had been born with.

A deadly, invisible, incurable disease—much like the virus that was claiming its due today. And it lay in our names.

Begum Farzana Sheikh. Mohammad Jameel Sheikh.

I screamed from under my grave, but no one heard me.

They'd buried me too far away. Just to be 'safe'.

(Based on a true story)

VIRUS-VIRUS

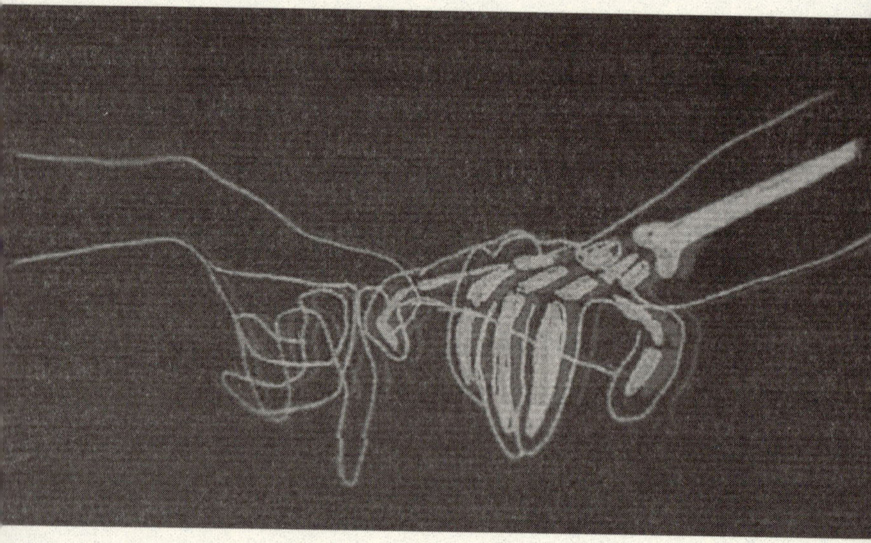

A VIRTUAL REALITY GAME PLAYED AND MADE POPULAR BY *the kids in the 'Corona Colonies' of the 2020s. The* ***Coronavirus disease 2019 (COVID-19)*** *was an infectious disease that was first identified in December 2019 in Wuhan, China, but spread within months to over 200 countries affecting more than 3.6 million people globally. The exact number of fatalities from the disease is still unknown.*

(Sing to the tune of 'Ringa Ringa Roses')

ShhhhhShhhhhhShhhhhhhh
It Creep Creep Creeps
Silently,
It Reap Reap Reaps

You have it
You pass it

Atchooo-Coughh
For the masses

Wash it!!!

Wipe it!!!

We're all Quarantined!!!

THE COVID CUPBOARD

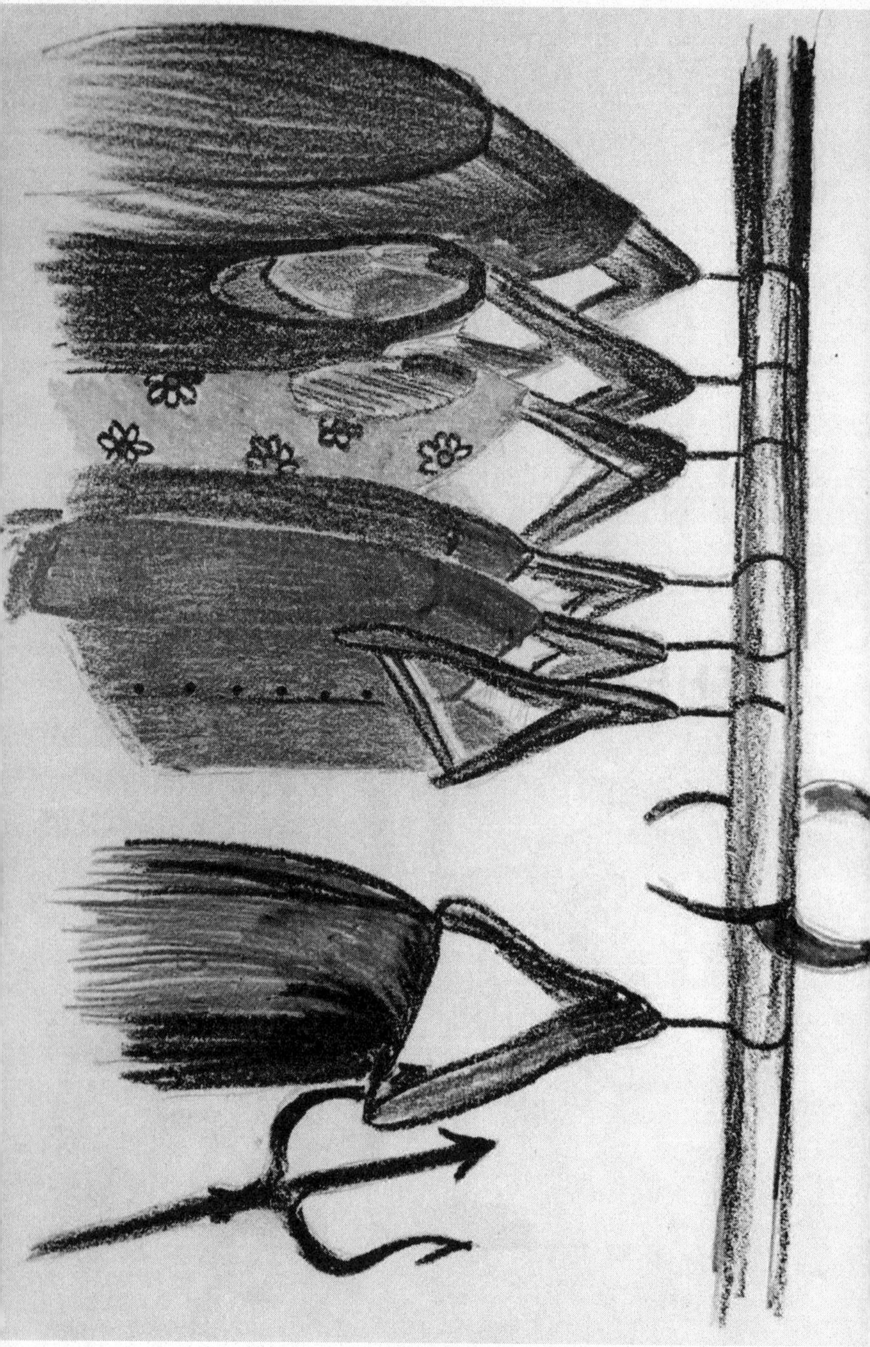

JUNE 2020, GLAMUP MAGAZINE, DIGITAL EDITION 13

Contd. from pg 5

Top 20 Lockdown Innovative Inventions
No. 4: Karishma's Special Covid Cupboard

Karishma Khanna's Covid Cupboard idea is simple but packs a punch. Rather than using her room-size walk-in wardrobe, Karishma used her mind and downgraded to one small special cupboard in the first week of lockdown itself. 'The Covid Cupboard,' as she calls it, 'is filled with clothes I've never worn, but have always wanted to. Comfortable, loose, cool day clothes and a bunch of sexy nightwear.' *GlamUp Magazine* spoke to her about her innovative idea.

Advantages

No wasting time browsing through your entire collection before deciding what you want to wear to stay home. Plus, once lockdown ends you can pack away your special Covid Collection and donate it to the needy.

'*Aam ke aam, gutliyon ke daam,*' says Karishma.

Challenges

'So, I had initially planned on giving my Covid Clothes to the squatters down the street, but then some friends told me they've gone. The roads are bereft of the homeless and the poor, I mean, there aren't even any beggars left. They've all been packed into trains and sent home, or put away in some state-run camps outside the city borders. Essential, I guess, in these times to keep the city folk safe. I was disappointed but I didn't let that get in my way.

'Figured if the squatters and beggars (bless their souls) never returned, I'd just make dust cloths of my Covid Clothes. Or maybe send them off to orphanages. There will always be orphans in the world, won't there?' she told us.

The eternal optimist in Karishma believes she will cross that bridge when she comes to it. After all, no good deed ever goes unpunished. Someone, somewhere is waiting to receive from her. Of that she is sure.

And so are we.

For now, Karishma has let go of all her Sita *bais* and Ram *bhaiyas* and is using this time to detoxify and explore parts of herself she'd never known existed. Dancing, playing the piano, baking, and painting the most complex designs on ceramics. 'Maybe one of these will fuel a future business idea, who knows? For the brave new world of tomorrow holds in its womb a limitless ocean of opportunities. And I for one am just getting started,' signs off the vivacious mother of a naughty one-year old.

Congratulations again, Karishma Khanna on being featured in the *Top 20 Lockdown Innovative Inventions List. GlamUp Magazine* and its partner groups are proud to be associated with you.

We're watching you, girl!

More power to Staying Happy, Staying In.

#StayHome#StaySafe
#NoPlaceBetterThanHome

Updated June 2021

Karishma was right about her Covid Collection.

Her Covid Clothes did get used.

Designer body bags were made out of them.

We at *GlamUp* salute every life lost in the Pandemic Riots, 2020.

#StayHome#StaySafe

ANNAPURNA

A BOUQUET OF USELESS TALENTS LAY UNUSED IN Annapurna's life. She'd never had the time to use them nor the gumption to try. Her eldest brother, Vijju, had taught her once to ride a bicycle under the shade of the fiery chinar trees in Srinagar. She had been about nine at the time when the whole Mishra clan had travelled together from Delhi to attend a distant relative's wedding and stayed on for the rest of the month. They had needed an entire railway bogey for the journey, she remembered, but most other memories from the trip had faded away.

Except for the day she'd sat on the bicycle for the very first time. That day she remembered vividly, the unusual sweltering summer afternoon when their Amma, a strict powerhouse of useful talent, had given Annapurna and her sister some time off from their daily chores. 'Run along, you two, we'll continue with the lessons in the evening,' she'd said before disappearing quietly into their Baba's bedroom. She'd locked the door behind her with a definitive click, something she didn't do very often, that click resounded in the silence of the afternoon. Perhaps Amma had needed a nap. Annapurna wasn't sure but the thing she knew for certain was that every talent their Amma had taught the sisters that summer had served them well, just as their Amma had promised, their whole lives through. And yet despite the usefulness of the talents they had gathered that summer, what remained unforgettable in Annapurna's mind was the feeling of being astride that bike many sizes too large for her that careless afternoon. A useless talent she had honed over many nights of stolen moon over the month the family had spent there.

Yes, she had hidden from them and perfected her balancing skills until she could ride the cycle completely by herself. Cycles that had thick steel rods in front between the handlebars and the seat, were only for men, she knew, and yet she, a little girl of nine, had managed somehow to stay on. Stood firmly on her feet and swung a leg over the side, then she was off and away, pedalling hard down the lane. Sadly, that was the last time she had been allowed to do either—ride a cycle or stand on her own feet.

As summer drained to monsoon, Annapurna slowly started grasping how many things in life were reserved 'For Men Only'. Owning a sense of humour was one of them. She was so petrified of having another one of her useless talents snatched away that she told no one of its existence. Her own little secret that was meant for her alone, she kept it masked from the gaze of men. Much like the pads she kept hidden even after her period had passed. They had been trained well, the sisters, in 'The Dark Arts of Conceal All', and no one knew better than them of the unicorns that existed only in the lives of little girls. However, the trouble was that Annapurna's bone of funny was no unicorn—it was real and it was badass and it would not stay curbed. Truth be told, she didn't want it getting stale either so she kept it in use in the most unexpected ways. Blowing into it bubbles of hope and light that made it twinkle through the dullest of nights.

Come autumn, she ground her sense of humour into a coarse grainy mixture and used it generously in the strangest ways. She put a pinch of it into her *kathal achar* along with the powdered *rai* and *kalonji* to turn her special pickle just a wee bit more sour. She crushed it in with the green pistachios before she set them free in the sweet syrupy ocean that surrounded her golden *malpuas*. Her *malpuas* were known in her family and *mohalla* for the crunch they carried in their hearts. The secret to that crunch lay in her secret ingredient, and she didn't limit the use of it to just food! Sometimes for fun she added a dash of it into the *neel* with which she starched the shirts of the menfolk. Made them stiff as cardboard, her sense of humour did! And then sometimes she'd make a chutney with it too—add *nimbu hari mirch* and *dhania* and pound all of it together on her favourite black *silbatta*. This special chutney she'd save and serve on multiple occasions to all the little girls whom she met at festivals or even otherwise. She believed the chutney made them sharp-witted, got them good lives and homes, it did. And her *silbatta* gained from that wicked powder too, it developed its own super power, even the bluntest knife sharpened on it turned razor sharp. And it works with the same precision even now.

She is eighty-five now and still no one knows what useless talents she clutches within and the secret ways she uses them. Annapurna, that is her name.

Once, very long ago, she'd been born to a surname too, not the one she holds now, this came from her husband. I speak of the one she had belonged to—by birth. Of course, that had come to her from her Baba and his father must have carried it before. Come to think of it, she never asked her own Amma what her surname had been before she'd met Baba. In a way, you could say, her own mother she never knew. An identity mangled in a heap of many words, much like her own. Daughter, Sister, Mother, Wife. *Dadi, Masi, Bua, Chachi, Chooha.* So many lives she had lived and yet of them she was none. In many frames she lay with identities cut and pasted upon her. Choice had never been an option for her, you see.

Now, after eighty-five years of having lived these names, they had turned irrelevant almost overnight. Mother, Aunt, Wife. WIDOW. All nothing but empty words that lay cluttered in the porch outside her front door. For in the face of the pandemic, all relationships had turned quite meaningless. Not one person from the squiggly family chart that life had drawn up for her could be with her in this time. 'Too risky,' they said, her two sons with families of their own. Yes, I guess everyone was petrified of catching the Virus.

Now she was in the winter of her life and lived alone atop a higgledy-piggledy crumbling house, that in structure resembled the current architecture of her teeth. Brown and molten like chocolate left out in the sun too long. Her home had been melting for many years now but her boys, blinded perhaps by worries of their own, could not see the rivulets of wax gathering outside their childhood home. She waded through it all the time by herself, so she knew. Up and down those steep stone steps that had once held on their bare skin Annapurna's *baraat* of more than one hundred. Now those steps lay crumbling, much like the meandering alleyways of Daryaganj where she lived. Every crinkle on her face told a story, every wrinkle in its depth held a sigh unfulfilled. There were so many tales from her youth just waiting to be heard, but she never had anyone around to hear them.

In this pandemic too she was alone and yet for a change she wasn't, her younger sister Chhoti had come to stay with her. The most talkative of them all, she'd been as a child. She had come to visit Annapurna a few weeks before the pandemic hit and now she was stuck, unable to get home—not her own home, she didn't have one, the home that belonged to whichever one of her children she was spending the season with.

The family that was to host her this season had a pre-planned vacation to take and so they had sent her off to her elder sister's home. Until they could call her back, of course, but that didn't happen. Wasn't their fault the lockdown hit, they couldn't call her back even after they managed to return home.

Now on a single bed they lay with a tangled maze of white hair in their midst, the sisters! Yes, they truly were quite a sight, Annapurna may even have cracked a joke or two on their withered state, but she feared her Chhoti could not laugh anymore. She had fallen deathly silent, lying on the bed all day, staring blankly out of the lone window on the opposite wall, not moving, not saying a single word. It seemed like a combination of diabetes and life had sucked her soul away. Annapurna just didn't know how she could help, they couldn't even step out. The rules regarding restricted movement of senior citizens were very strict and there was no one around to help. Their kids called on WhatsApp every day, they were good that way, transferred money to them and all, but as the days passed Annapurna realised their reassurances were much like those of the government and people in power—meaningless. *'Aatmanirbhar'* was the new way to be. The new mantra to happiness. She understood now in her heart of hearts that through Lockdowns, the Unlocks and for many months beyond, until this dreaded disease was brought to its knees, she and Chhoti would have to live alone. *Aatmanirbhar* is what they'd have to be.

The tenant lady who lived on the ground floor had been helpful to them, of course. Had brought them groceries the last few weeks, small plastic packets filled with veggies, *arhar dal* and *parimal* rice that she left midway up the stairs. But she could do no more than that, for their safety and her own. She could not help them with their daily chores and their regular maid could no longer come. So every morning Annapurna with her rickety bones woke up at the crack of dawn. She cleaned and scrubbed and swept all day, cooked the food and washed the dishes before she finally sat down to pray. All this she did for three months, while Chhoti continued to lie silently on the bed.

Then one day Annapurna woke up at noon, something she had never done before. She cursed herself for sleeping late. That's when something bizarre struck her. There was no one around to question why she had slept so late. Chhoti just lay silently on her side of the bed. For the first time, there was no one to question her about *anything*, nothing she had to do.

No maids, no sons, no relatives. No buses, no planes, no railways. No temples, no sabhas, no jagrans. No responsibilities of any kind at all. There was nothing of her old life left anymore so in that moment she decided she should turn new too. Change herself into a new person for a lark. She could you know, I told you she was special, one of her other hidden talents was Imagination!

She felt bad about not being able to help her sister though, and then suddenly in her mind an idea most preposterous grew. Perhaps the germ of this idea came from her wicked sense of humour but this isn't something I can confirm. Anyway, here's what happened next.

All her life Annapurna had been taught to never step out, not even from the bathroom, without her blouse and petticoat but today she took them off and walked across the room. Naked, bare-breasted and free to the trunk in the corner. From the painted steel trunk with the vermilion swastika on its chest, she pulled out two pairs of pants and two starched white-collared shirts. Chhoti sat up for the first time in all the weeks she'd been there, and stared at her sister, horrified. Annapurna ignored her shocked look and continued rummaging through the large steel box and from it now she took out an old battered gramophone, some vinyl records, an unopened packet of beedis (Pardeshi Beedis, they were called) and a half-filled bottle of Old Monk rum. All things that had belonged to her husband once, she decided to put them now to good use. From them, with her power of wild imagination, she created a Magical Day of Firsts for Chhoti and herself.

The times were unusual, no doubt about that, and Annapurna decided the sisters should use it to do something they had never in their lives done. Ride the 'For Men Only' cycles of their minds, unashamed and unafraid with no one around who would judge them. So with a steel glass of rum and a beedi in her hand, she turned to Chhoti and said, 'Let's try living free for a change. Let's make this time count. Take my hand, Chhoti, let's not miss this ride!'

Chhoti was shocked at first but then she giggled, remember I told you she'd been the spirited, talkative one? So she took her sister's hand and together they took a giant leap of faith. They threw caution to the winds that had always pushed them back and for a change enjoyed themselves to the hilt!

They discarded their white saris and put on the shirts and pants Annapurna had taken out. They pulled out the playing cards that had been kept away. They didn't cook or eat or pray that day. Yes, they behaved like debauched men. It was fun and mad and in all that insanity they even missed the phone calls from their kids. It was a day of firsts for the sisters. They danced and sang with all their might and when the battered old gramophone gave up they began to sing their own songs!

'Aaaja aajaaa main hun pyaar teraaaaa....'

They sang at the top of their lungs as they sipped on their rum, smoked their beedis and ate *chivda.* And later in the evening when Annapurna walked to the window to draw the curtains and put on the night light, she saw in the lane outside people much younger than them walking about stifled and suffocated not just by masks or the gloves they wore but by their shackled minds. They looked tired, worn out and scared of an unseen evil that lurked between them. Strangely, Annapurna was no longer scared, she and Chhoti had found a sense of independence that now they would never lose.

So in this Lockdown while everyone in the world outside struggled to find a meaning to their lives, the ladies discovered freedom of the truest kind. If you strain your ears you may hear them even now. The two old ladies with their white hair swinging, their bodies sashaying in rhythm, singing in their raspy voices songs of exploration.

I'm not sure what will happen to the young ones outside but I believe the sisters will weather this storm. For you see, up in their tower of total independence the ladies are like Rapunzels lost in their own spell.

Now you may wonder how I know all of this. Let's just say I know because I've lived with Annapurna through her married years. I was around before that too, though I'm not sure how long I will exist after she's gone—not with the way things have been going so far. No one but her cares that I'm crumbling, they're breaking, remaking and renovating many like me. I was young once, much like her long ago, but today outsiders only see my façade. I'm the house into which Annapurna was married, the crumbling steps that run through are my veins and I promise to keep the sisters safe in my embrace as long as I possibly can. Just as she has not abandoned me all these years, I will stick by her as long as I can.

PANDEMIC BLANKET

THAT BLANKET WAS ENCHANTED, MAGICAL, I HAD always thought. With its many splashes of colour amidst that ocean of grey, it held within it much more than it was ever ready to reveal. I remember hiding behind the curtain when I was little, watching my mother go through the yearly winter routine of getting the blanket out to 'breathe'. Every year on the twenty-first of November, she would bring down the old painted trunk which held many of her myriad treasures from the attic, and take out her most precious possession, the gorgeous 'Pandemic Blanket'. The one her mother, my grandmother, had woven during the Great Pandemic of 2019. Now, anyone who had known my mother would tell you that she was hard as nails, wasn't known for her sentimentality, that's for sure. And yet, for the two weeks that the blanket came out, she would change. How exactly is difficult to explain, let's just say she became lighter, more filled with life and yes, laughter. I turned fifty-five this January, and this had been the winter routine in our home, ever since I can remember, until of course my mother breathed her last, four days ago. Today is the twenty-fifth of November and the blanket is now mine to keep.

The twenty-first of November had been the day of my grandmother's birth, maybe that's why it earmarked the cusp between the normal and the exceptional. For, in those two glorious winter weeks each year, my mother, otherwise quite the disciplinarian, abandoned all rules and let the whole family live free. 'Do whatever you want,' she said. This two-week special rule applied to everything from the food we ate, to the time we slept to the work we did. Anything could be done, or not done with guiltless aplomb.

My sister and I looked forward to this time of year not just for the indiscipline (which was an added perk) but for the stories. For every night of those two weeks, our mother would hold us close in the embrace of that warm woollen blanket and tell us tales of a time gone by. In her whispery voice she would speak of people and places that had once lived but now lay buried in the sands of time. And as we huddled by her side wrapped in the warmth of that huge blanket, we could almost see every story she told unfold before our eyes like on a giant theatre screen. The blanket held us tight, as if every thread in its every patch strained to have us miss not one word uttered that night. But, to be honest, as a small child, the Pandemic Blanket was quite intimidating for me. Scary even, especially that ragged silver white patch that ran through it, never quite fitting in. Like a giant scar racing across the face of a beautiful woman. Ugly yet distinct. Unsightly yet necessary.

I remember the first time I saw the white patch, one of those cold winter afternoons, when I was about five. I had been playing *chor-police* with my cousins out in the garden and had wandered into my mother's semi-darkened room to hide. The blanket lay on the edge of her bed, a sliver of the sun's rays falling on it through the drawn curtains, when suddenly I felt it move. Felt, not saw, it stretch out, make itself just a wee bit more comfortable as it basked languidly in the warmth of the afternoon sun. I know it could have been my mind playing tricks but two things happened in that moment. One, I spotted for the first time that unsightly patch of white, and two, I promised myself I'd never be alone with that blanket again. 'And yet here we are,' I thought today, eyeing it with trepidation as it lay innocently at the bottom of my mother's bed just as it had that winter afternoon so many years ago. We watched each other with caution, neither knowing quite what to do.

The blanket was unusual, no doubt about that, it had a voice of its own. It spoke wordlessly and refused to be silenced. Perhaps it was all the patterns it had woven into it, like a gigantic jigsaw puzzle with hundreds of pieces that shifted and fell into place differently every time the blanket moved. It made you believe in the extraordinary. *A magenta pink daisy emerged from a bright scarlet moon and merged with the deep navy blue seas that lay filled with glowing marigold plankton.* Yes, my grandmother's Pandemic Blanket was no ordinary quilt, it held within it dreams of endless possibilities and nightmares of the darkest night.

Like I said, my grandmother had stitched it during the Great Pandemic of 2019 when, the Covid-19 as it came to be known was ravaging the world, bringing all of humanity crawling to its knees. Confining people across the globe to their homes for months on end without hope of normal life ever returning. That Pandemic had served as a great lesson to mankind—that there truly was no better friend and no bigger foe than Mother Earth, her smallest sigh enough to sweep many dynasties of men to dust. The blanket spoke of that, and much more besides. My grandmother had made it from memories that lived deep within her soul. She had woven into each patch of the blanket a story of its own and then stitched them all together to make a greater whole.

People who knew her said she had become a bit loony about the blanket. It had started to consume her. Once she started to stitch, so the story went, she could not stop. It demanded completion, like a greedy, insatiable beast that commanded being fed, at any cost. At least that's what she told everyone, but then she'd also been one of the greatest storytellers in the world. It wasn't her kohl-lined grey-green eyes or her shining olive skin or even the inky black curls that cascaded down her back that made her unforgettable, it was the sharpness of her words. They cut you like a knife thrust deep into the heart, her writing took your breath away. She had been one of the most brilliant writer-poets of her time, knitting together stories filled with fascinating characters caught in the most crazy, fantastical lives. And she loved it, loved living in a make-believe world filled only with her words. Until everything stopped.

My mother told me that when she was about fourteen, if she lay silently in her room, even with her door shut, she could hear the tip-tapping of her mother's ferocious fingers sweeping across the keyboard, consuming with a gluttonous hunger, reams and reams of virtual paper. She had been a bit obsessive that way, my grandmother. Brilliant. Passionate. And perhaps just a little mad.

And then one day, a few months after the Pandemic hit, her words dried up, just like that, Poof! And they were gone. A drought of stories so cruel it gobbled my grandmother's voice and left her lost in a forest of deep stony silence. No one could rouse her from it, there was no way out. Her husband and daughter both tried but to no avail, nothing compelled her to write anymore. I'm told she tried, several times, to get her words to talk but the advent of the Pandemic and all that it brought in its wake, made her stories seem pointless. Irrelevant even. Real life had turned stranger than fiction, how could she possibly tell a tale better than that? Her grey-green eyes grew colder now, her fingers aching to appease her raging mind but whenever she sat in front of her computer screen, she drew a blank. She was bursting at the seams with stories that couldn't be told, like an over-roasted tomato that needed desperately to be pulled off the stove. She didn't know what to do. And so, she started to knit.

Savagely she knitted with the yarn her mother had left behind, stories of her past and her present too. Patches filled with colours, and each colour held a tale. Of her dreams and desires and so much else. And when she started running out of her own stories she turned to others for inspiration. She whispered into the patches now, stories of her neighbours and their loved ones. She wove in tales of the watchman's secret night life, the cook's cheating wife, what her self-righteous neighbour had done one summer long ago, and even the short little man she'd once met who turned out to be a thief. All day she knitted at a frenetic pace, patches and patterns that jostled for space in the biggest masterpiece of her life.

After telling tales of people she did not stop.

She wove in stories of her doorbell,
Of the fingers that had rung it
And the tales that it could tell.

All the houses she had lived in,
And all the walls she'd seen,
And she stitched in all the people,
Who within those walls had been.

Some patches that were beautiful
And others ugly were born,
Each held a life of its own,
Each sang its own swansong.

And then the unthinkable happened. She started to run out of yarn. All the shops were closed and no one was doing deliveries. Knitting was not counted amongst the essential services. She knew not what to do so she started to undo every piece of knitwear she possessed, every colour, every hue. She undid all her old sweaters, her mufflers and even all the shawls. Then she wound all the yarn into a great big ball and started anew. Her husband and daughter stood by horrified, that's when it dawned on them that she had finally crossed over, from their world into one from which there was no return.

With eyes now blazing with a fiery light she knitted deep into the night. She could not stop, she would not stop even when the new yarn got over. She sat heaving with desperation now, she still had so much more to say. 'But how to say it,' she thought. 'All the thread has gone.' She moved around the house until she found a bath rug and into the blanket it went.

The rug spoke of footprints of all
Who in the bathroom had been,
It sang aloud stories
Of things no one had ever seen.

She wove her precious stories with lace from the curtains that hung on her windows, she pulled out the threads from the embroidered cushion covers, she even unravelled a tapestry her great grandmother had made, a family heirloom. In this way my grandmother's Pandemic Blanket grew in length and breadth and memory, it crept and sighed and moved in ways beyond imagination. And then one day she realized there truly was not a thread left.

That's when her eyes fell on her own unruly head. Her hair had turned white since she had begun on the blanket and it flowed down her back in a silvery stream. Yes, this would certainly do. So she took a pair of scissors to her head, and cut off every bit of her hair. She wound the long strands into a silken ball, silkier than any yarn she'd used, then out came her knitting needles and she began her task again.

That's the story we were told, when we cuddled into that blanket. Of all the patches and what they meant, of all the stories she had woven in. My grandmother, the greatest storyteller of all time. It was her own silvery white hair that held all those stories together, that's what had she had used to finally join up all the patches. Our family Pandemic Blanket, the most precious gift we shared.

I walked slowly to the blanket, touched its every patch. It seemed to be lying quite still today. Maybe it understood my mother had gone. I picked it up and wrapped it around myself, and as I did, I heard it speak to me, heard it whisper words of comfort. I knew then what I had to do. Keep it safe for my kin, for the generations that would come after me, for it held within itself, all the Stories of Us and who someday we may be. The blanket held me and I slipped gently into its embrace, the white patch that had once seemed ugly and out of place transforming now into the lifeline with which the blanket breathed.

(Based on a true story)

THE PEACH:
A MODERN FAIRYTALE

ONCE UPON A TIME IN A LAND FAR FAR AWAY, THERE lived a giant peach which was inhabited by all kinds of creatures. There were worms and maggots and flies and ants and when the tides ran high there were some fish folk that visited too. For once in a blue moon the inhabitants of the peach witnessed the waters, they didn't know where the waters came from and didn't know where they went. After all, the rest of the year the tides ran low and life went on just fine. The water days were a tad tough, or rough you may say—for the peach would shake violently and the earthquake would wreak havoc in the homes of its inhabitants. But no one really cared, after all, what's a few bad days in a lifetime. And why must one focus on the negatives, there was always so much to look forward to.

The ants went for runs on the surface of the peach, and the maggots burrowed tunnels deep into its centre. And the flies! The flies buzzed busily all over the peach—why, a couple of the braver ones had even flown through the tunnels built by the maggots and visited the very centre of the universe! These were wonderful, exploratory, exciting times, each morning brought for the inhabitants a grand new adventure and the evenings, a time to celebrate! Oh! How they would dance, sing and make merry sipping the sweet nectar of the peach with their straws as they regaled each other with stories of their day and planned for the bright sunny skies of tomorrow! Life was perfect actually, save the fish folk who when they visited, whispered warnings of a doom to come. 'Your world will end if you don't look beyond,' they said. '*Youmusnotwaste, youmusnotplunder, youmuspayheed, yourworldgoesunder*', '*youmusnotwaste, youmusnotplunder, muspayheed, yourworldgoesunder*', over and over and over again. But the inhabitants could not understand them, perhaps they never really tried. The wise ants who had been around forever said it didn't matter what the fish folk believed. 'They're doomsayers, outsiders, what do they know? They don't live on our peach. We've been here forever and the world has never ended. It never will. Live free. Be wild.'

Next morning, the half-eaten rotting peach, which had been hanging precariously at the edge of the rock for the last week, fell into the rock pool. A giant wave washed over it.

The End

ACKNOWLEDGEMENTS

STORIES NEED THEIR LISTENERS, JUST AS RABBITS NEED their leaves! One can't possibly exist sans the other.

This would've been impossible without you: Siddharth, my dearest husband and biggest partner in crime, who heard and reheard every story until they were pouring out of his ears. You are my inspiration, mummy, pet snake and Ginormous Grump all rolled into one.

My most delightfully insane family: My mother, Preeti Gill, the wind beneath my wings, thank you for teaching me the power of belief. None of us were possible without you. My younger sister, biggest critic and closest confidante, Bani Gill. The one person who knows where each of these stories originate. Actually, she's privy to all my original tales. My father, K.S. Daddy Gill, my anchor. Rarely seen until I set sail, and yet always there to ground me when I need it most. Thank you, Papa.

My three best friends: Jaya Misra, my badass elder sister and love beyond infinity, and Tanusri Dasgupta and Ipsita Deb, my most precious gems, for their invaluable feedback. Thank you all for getting me to continue writing, even if it was for 'our own' entertainment those first few weeks of lockdown.

Brijesh Jacob, who gave me a perfect title for this book! You and yours are to us our family away from home. But you know that already!

Niyati Singh, for giving my words physical shape. You go, girl!

My closest girl pals: Ritti Chopra and Dipika Bajpai. My Unquestioning Forevers.

And all the Apocalyptic WhatsApp friend folk who rallied beside me all the way: Sur, Praks, Vani, Maria, Mini. Your feedback meant the world.

My college friends who emerged from the woodwork and did some big rah rahs along the road:

Dhruv, Silky, Mitsy, Auro, Pram, Bratman, Goa, Dundee, Nimit, DivK, Akshat.

And all the others who read these stories on groups and stayed with me throughout.

My editor, Renuka Chatterjee, who plucked these stories from my wildest imagination and made them a reality. Thank you, Renuka.

And thank you Speaking Tiger and Ravi Singh for believing in me and taking these lockdown tales on.

Here's hoping I've done justice to your collective belief.

PS. I forgot to mention some members of my delightfully mismanaged squiggly household. My beautiful children, Rohaan and Raaya, my crazy dogs, Bashira and Zed, and most importantly, Prema and Rajesh, who make my chaos complete. Thank you for all the noise and commotion, that sometimes helps dull the painful realities.

I hope we leave for you a brighter, better future beyond The Day After Tomorrow!